She should n[...]
close...

The babe's essence was so small and tender and warm, but the essence of the man, so large and powerful and arrogant—and hot—brought her to her knees.

"Angelo," Isobel murmured.

She wanted him to be mortal, to comfort her, to take her into his arms and make love to her till hell froze over and the triumph of good over evil was no longer at stake.

But she knew that was not possible, and she pretended it didn't matter. "Stay with him a little longer? I just want to go...to the kitchen."

"Whatever you want, Iso, you can have right here."

"You mean you'll conjure it?" She barely prevented herself from bursting into hysterical laughter. He would not conjure the only thing she truly wanted. "No. I can't have what I want right here."

"Then go." His voice was deeper, harsher than she had ever known. If he knew what was in her heart and her thoughts, then it had reason to be. She wanted more than anything to be away from him, where she could envision a life without him. "Seth and I will be fine," he said, cradling the baby to his chest.

And so will I, she thought fiercely. *So will I, when you are gone and all that is left for me is Seth.*

Dear Reader,

Last year we brought you a quartet of
AVENGING ANGELS—the sexiest angels this side
of heaven, to be exact. And you loved them so
much that we're bringing you two more of these
very special heroes.

Whenever there is injustice, the Avenging Angels
are on the case, ready to right the wrong but often
not ready to deal with the pleasures of the flesh.

Carly Bishop, who was one of the originating
authors of the quartet, is back with Angelo's story.
This *Angel with an Attitude* is about to learn a
thing or two about life and love.

Next month be sure to look for *A Real Angel* by
Cassie Miles.

We're delighted we could bring you more
AVENGING ANGELS!

Regards,

Debra Matteucci
Senior Editor & Editorial Coordinator
Harlequin Books
300 East 42nd Street
New York, NY 10017

Angel with an Attitude
Carly Bishop

Harlequin Books

TORONTO • NEW YORK • LONDON
AMSTERDAM • PARIS • SYDNEY • HAMBURG
STOCKHOLM • ATHENS • TOKYO • MILAN
MADRID • WARSAW • BUDAPEST • AUCKLAND

ISBN 0-373-22440-0

ANGEL WITH AN ATTITUDE

Copyright © 1997 by Cheryl McGonigle

This edition published by arrangement with Harlequin Books S.A.

® and TM are trademarks of the publisher. Trademarks indicated with
® are registered in the United States Patent and Trademark Office, the
Canadian Trade Marks Office and in other countries.

Printed in U.S.A.

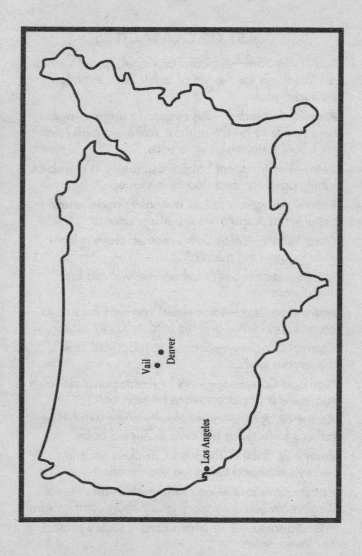

Vail · · Denver

· Los Angeles

CAST OF CHARACTERS

Isobel Avedon —A guardian angel, Isobel would risk anything for the life of baby Seth, even her immortal soul.

Angelo de Medici —An avenging angel, Angelo held justice to be the highest value, until his love for Isobel taught him otherwise.

Seth —The innocent babe was caught in a web of family passions and deadly intrigue.

Pascal —Angelo's fellow avenging angel knew better what Angelo would finally choose.

Gina Sellers —Was Seth's mother playing both ends against the middle?

Ian Candless —Seth's father—he wanted his illegitimate son.

Bruce Candless —Ian's eldest son was a force to be reckoned with, and his mother's only ally.

Conrad Candless —Second son Conrad took a dangerous path.

Harrison Candless —Ian's brilliant, paranoid third son knew a photo op when he saw one.

Kelsey St. John —Ian's only daughter wanted her father's fortune for her own expected baby.

Emory St. John —The lead Candless attorney, Kelsey's husband loved her too much.

Patrice Candless —Ian's wife took in his illegitimate son with more grace than compassion.

Pilar Sanchez —Her green card couldn't protect her loved ones.

Chapter One

All that fateful day Isobel had sensed the threat of mortal danger to the baby Seth. She should have seen it coming, should have been able to prevent it, but she was looking for an accident, not a cold-blooded murder.

When the bullets from a drive-by shooting tore into tiny Seth's mother and dropped her like a stone to the pavement, Isobel caved in.

It wasn't as if she hadn't witnessed such unexpected, inhuman crimes. In another time and place, she had died of just such a heartless act as this young mother had.

But when the baby tumbled screaming from his mother's lifeless arms, Isobel's angelic sensibilities deserted her. She lost perspective. A fierce and tender emotion, unheard-of in a Guardian Angel, rose up in her angel consciousness. Something about tiny Seth stole the heart and soul of the guardian Isobel Avedon had become.

She could not have put a name to her fascination, nor any justification. She was, after all, five centuries into her angelic service to humankind. Thousands of babies had passed through her loving guardianship.

No one child was any less precious to her than the hundreds before or the one to follow—which was as it should be.

Part of her knew that. She was not little Seth's birth mother and never could be. She owed her allegiance and her powers and her love to all mankind.

Somehow, none of that mattered. All these centuries later, the memory of her own murder fueled the fire in her soul. It wasn't so much that her own life had been cut short, as it was that in dying before her time, she had never even imagined the face of her own offspring, never conceived one or nursed one at her breast, never rejoiced in his or her first words or steps.

Isobel Avedon had never even lain with her beloved.

Now, hundreds of years later, Isobel wanted this babe—and he needed a mother. If she were to be cast out from paradise for ever after, she would still do it, for in that terrible instant of his real mother's death, Isobel loved that child above all else.

This was, of course, forbidden.

The emotion took her by storm. She might have turned aside from such human feelings. She might have let them pass, might have chalked them up to a sweet and fleeting temporal aberration. She was a Guardian Angel, powerful enough to dissuade mortals—through sheer mind power—from committing illegal, cruel or thoughtless acts.

But Isobel had never in all her time as an angel known such a swift or urgent need to act outside her powers. There were no rules to guide her...save the one that forbade what she was about to do.

What she *must* do.

So Isobel acted on her feelings, and in the wake of her decision, she became fully, awkwardly human—plunging into the earthly dimension without finesse or any semblance of grace.

She had no plan, or the slightest concept of the consequences of materializing out of thin air into a human body.

She hadn't remembered what it was to assume human form. To be born again into the hellishness of human constraints. She knew nothing of the pain involved or what it was like to move on earth, how unbearably slow and plodding she would become.

She hadn't remembered what it was like to breathe, especially not air so thick and noxious she could scarcely drag a breath into her human lungs. Despite the loose flowing skirt and light silk tank top, her physical form weighed on her like the yoke on a beast of burden.

Weaker than the babe she intended to save, she sank to her knees beside the terror-stricken child. Every detail seemed frozen in time to her. The screams and shouts of onlookers. The ungodly roar of cars. The scent of death on the breeze lifting strands of Seth's dead mother's long blond hair.

Choking on his own cries, the babe strained toward his mother while her blood poured out onto the rough, cracked concrete sidewalk. Isobel's transition to her temporal form had cost her dearly. She had no strength to move in those first moments, much less to touch the babe, to comfort him.

He wore a tiny sweat suit and designer baby tennis shoes. A plump, healthy five-month-old, he had beautiful, shiny dark curls and enormous brown eyes. But as his mother lay lifeless, clumps of sparse grass poked him in his tiny mottled face, mocking his confusion and his rage.

The danger to Seth hadn't ended, either. The car carrying the murderers, a huge, shiny black monster, screeched to a halt fifty feet down the street, then whined as the driver backed up.

Deadly weapons poked out the windows, and the hideous crack of gunfire began again—and Isobel wondered if Hell could be any more horrifying than the violent tableau playing out before her now.

The murderers' return meant they intended to finish the job and kill tiny Seth too.

Onlookers shouted and dived for cover. Adolescents darted about with boxes that blared music that sounded to Isobel like nothing more than harsh, ugly sounds. Other cars slowed in curiosity and then sped away. Still, Isobel battled for the strength to move.

And the baby... The baby reaching for his mother—the tears, the shrill scream of terror, his tiny nose running, mouth drooling. He could crawl, but barely. He fell and stretched and rolled over, his little body twisting with rage.

She fought the terrifying earthbound sensations with all her might. She couldn't fail. Nothing mattered save plucking that precious baby out of harm's way.

With a burst of energy, she scooped up the baby and clutched him tight to her mortal body. He smelled of powdery talc and panicky tears. A wave of pure maternal love swept through Isobel. Heedless for just that second of the bullets flying through the air, she savored the sensation, the earthiness, the raw power of simply being alive.

Nothing in heaven or on earth could ever match

the power of a mother's love, or the feel of a baby in her arms—a sweet and needful baby clinging to her.

But when bullets began biting into the sidewalk, blasting shards of concrete, the danger of indulging herself in cradling little Seth finally penetrated Isobel's human mind. She didn't know what to do, where to flee. Stuck with a human consciousness now, she had no chance to make a careful plan.

Where to go?

Small crumbling tract houses lined one side of the street. Seth's mother had come out of one of them, but to run to any one of them would be to draw the danger with her. There was a park across the street, a pathetic excuse for a park, where the youngest barrio children swung on broken-down swings and climbed monkey bars, and the older ones bought street drugs on the sly.

She chose instead the empty, run-down churchyard behind her and half a block down the street.

She stood, instinctively crouching low. Heat rose off the street in sickening waves. The stench of clouds coming out of cars seemed to fill the air. Bullets strafed past her mortal body, but she couldn't dwell on the pandemonium surrounding her.

If only she could get to the church.

If she tried, she thought desperately, she could make it to the sanctuary.

Surely those murdering men would not dare follow her with their death-dealing weapons inside a house of God.

Drawing on instincts she had long forgotten, Isobel darted past the confused and angry bystanders toward the churchyard.

Fighting to breathe, she slogged through the hot, sticky, threatening atmosphere. Her angel self could move faster than a ray of sunlight, but her woman self could never outrun the deadly bullets of merciless killers.

She had forgotten real fear, but now, for Seth, she knew it to her core. Knew it so well in one split second, when a bullet ripped over the flesh of her right shoulder, mere inches from Seth's tiny head, that she could taste it.

Cradling his small, sweet head to her other shoulder, she dared a backward glance. The car pursuing her wrenched to the curb. Angry, determined men in black clothing and dark glasses spilled out of it, shooting without a care for the lives of innocent bystanders.

She made it to the churchyard, which was surrounded by a high chain-link fence. Bullets and obscenities cracked in the air. She clutched tiny Seth closer to her breast and ran for the gate.

Choked with tired bougainvillea and unkempt, waist-high weeds, the gate held fast. She wasn't used to dealing with obstacles on a physical plane, and a part of her still believed she could simply move *through* the gate.

She tried, believing this, but the vines scratched her face, and her arm slammed painfully into the chain links. Near to panic without her guardian abilities, still the flight-or-fight human hormones flooded her mortal body. She managed with some sort of primitive, superhuman strength to force open the latch and shove through into the churchyard.

Her clothing was damp with Seth's tears and drooling and the blood welling from her own wound.

Shouts and gunshots rang out over and over again,
blasting the air. Little Seth choked and screamed, and
rage—another all-too-human emotion she'd forgotten—crowded Isobel's fear. If she were an avenging
angel, she could have dealt with these evil men, but
she wasn't.

Isobel Avedon, back in her human form after so
many centuries, cradling the baby Seth, prayed hard,
and ran even harder.

GLANCING AT THE LIST of evil and immoral acts requiring the attention of an Avenging Angel, Angelo
spared a moment to acknowledge to himself that, for
all the natural beauty of the Pacific at the latitude of
Los Angeles, he sorely missed his Denver office.

He missed the Rocky Mountains in the distance—though what was distance to an angel?—west
of the city. He missed the ambience, the essential
friendliness of mortals there. In Denver, most of the
streets still rolled up by ten o'clock at night, something only an Avenging Angel could properly appre-
ciate, and yet the area, the mountains, was far from
a cultural wasteland.

On the contrary. He had a fondness—some would
say a weakness—for mortal art forms, for plays and
opera, for sculpture, and for music from clever rap
and country and western to Wagner and Brahms and
Sondheim. And though, as an avenger, he could roam
the earth in the blink of an eye, searching for the
finest performances anywhere, he favored the
world-class visiting symphonies in the spectacular
natural amphitheaters of Red Rocks and Vail, Aspen
and Ouray.

Colorado had no equal, unless he counted Italy, which was where he had left his mortal heart.

In another oddly human and poignant manner, Angelo missed his staff, in particular his so-called secretary, Grace. He didn't know why this should be true. Grace was a busybody, know-it-all angel. She'd been around the heavenly block more times than Methuselah. Grace believed that everyone was entitled to her opinion—not that she ever came straight out with it. He had simply found his agenda expertly and irrevocably arranged to reflect Grace's priorities.

They had gotten along together about as well as jackals in the wild, but Angelo respected her bedrock principles above all others, and that was saying a great deal among angels. Her strength and her unending compassion—even her blessed opinions—mattered more to him than he wanted to admit.

So back at the Denver branch of Avenging Angels, he knew, Grace was in charge, if not in name, then by virtue of her opinions and her formidable organizational skills. All the same, he wished she had come with him to Los Angeles, where the International Avenging Angels ran its unwieldy operation.

He could have used her sense of perspective.

Or maybe he'd been too long about the business of assigning the avengers.

Scowling, he looked again to the cases requiring his attention. Pascal, titular head of the Los Angeles division of International, and the one who had called for Angelo's assistance, nodded.

He knew the backlog was terrible. So bad that even Saint Michael, patron saint of cops, had himself been passing out avenger assignments to ease the incredible burden. International trafficking in the illegal, the depraved and the corrupt plagued humankind on the eve of the twenty-first century.

Angelo took it personally.

Pascal repeated his oft-shared gratitude for Angelo's assistance in this time of crisis. "I've needed you, my friend. You see that now. You see for yourself how troubled is the City of Angels. Sorely troubled."

"Time for another flood of forty days and forty nights," Angelo joked darkly.

"A fresh start, so to speak?" Pascal concurred. "But of course, there was the covenant."

Angelo stifled a harsh response. He thrived on justice and lacked compassion—and he knew it. Rainbows were the metaphor for the covenant Pascal referred to, God's promise never to flood the entire earth again. But Angelo thought there must be two sides to a covenant. If there had been, mankind hadn't lived up to its end very well. Evil and wickedness were alive and well and flourishing on Planet Earth, and everywhere, Avenging Angels fell further and further behind.

Angelo dismissed his own dark thoughts. Despair wasn't a becoming attribute for an Avenging Angel—or any angel, for that matter. He took the matter of his attributes quite seriously. If he lacked compassion, it was because justice was so often thwarted. But in his essence, he knew that miracles transcend the laws of time and space. The Avenging Angels played a vital role he would never forsake, no matter how desperate the times, how seemingly hopeless the chore.

He often reminded himself of the old mortal say-

ing, that the darkness was always greatest before the
dawn—and dawn must soon arrive.

Still, a strange, quaintly human anxiety had been
stalking his consciousness like a shark circling nearer
and nearer its prey.

Pascal, always alert to the most fleeting impres-
sions, noticed Angelo's distraction. "What is it, my
friend?"

Angelo shook his head. "I don't know." Five centuries had passed since the last time such anxiety set
upon him.

Pascal turned his attention away from the small
mountain of injustices demanding an Avenging Angel, focusing all his considerable faculties upon Angelo. "Tell me," he urged.

Each of them knew every detail of the other's history, even their mortal lives, so all his friend could
be asking for was what lay between the lines, the
nuances, the matters of the human heart. Pascal was
as French in his angelic sensibilities as he had been
in his mortal life as a leader of the French Resistance
in the Second World War.

But then, Angelo had been an Italian prince in his
mortal life, more fiery, hot-blooded and passionate
than any overweening Frenchman by far.

Pascal smiled and shrugged elaborately for an angel without form. The two were old hands at these
harmless, macho human vanities. "Will you play
these games all day, my friend, or will you reveal
your true self?" he asked with a patience that galled
Angelo endlessly.

His remark irritated Angelo on another level as
well. Pascal didn't believe it possible for human beings to reveal their "true" selves—or even to tell the

truth at all, since he himself had never done so as a mortal.

But this was Pascal's charm. Angelo gazed out upon the Pacific, wishing it was instead his view of the Rockies. At last he answered the question. "I was thinking I have rarely been so...uneasy."

Pascal's focus narrowed still more. "Since Isobel was about to be murdered?" he asked.

"Yes." Angelo nodded without form. He went much further back than Pascal in his mortal life, and Isobel Avedon was his only story. "I loved her more than life. Shakespeare himself could not have dreamed or penned such a passion." In his soul-mind, no couple, not Romeo and Juliet or Tristan and Isolde, not Lancelot and Guinevere or even Katherina and Petruchio, held a candle to the love of Angelo and Isobel. Ill-fated, yes. Angelo had been the target of an assassin's knife, and Isobel...Dear God.

Isobel.

Images of her plight came to him, images so powerful and immediate he felt swallowed up whole, knew he was seeing her in the present moment. He saw her witnessing the seedy Los Angeles neighborhood...her incredible focus on the baby...the woman murdered on the street...the baby falling from its mother's arms.

And then Angelo watched as Isobel plunged out of her heavenly dimension and into a human form. A howling protest formed in his soul, but he had no power to stop her.

Isobel.

In all the ages, there had never been a woman so precious to Angelo as Isobel Avedon, but she was a heavenly being now, and her monumental foolishness in hurtling into the earthly dimension filled him with a terrible anger.

She was a Guardian Angel, and she should never again have been in such mortal danger. Her reckless actions changed all that, and the howling inside him pitched higher. She could suffer and die, and for no good reason. There were many, many ways she might have protected the baby's life without doing what she had done.

As hastily as she had gone over the edge into her human form, Angelo departed the company of his compatriot, Pascal, and moved to protect her from what evil pursued her in the earthly dimension. He spread his mighty wings, and in a burst of energy he was there, hovering above her in the barrio church-yard.

Isobel was fully mortal now. She could bleed— was bleeding. Oddly afraid to look closely at her, Angelo, who feared nothing and no one, who had taken on the worst humanity had to offer countless times in his service as an Avenging Angel, was afraid.

He feared distraction if he looked at her, and more…he feared his own feelings for a mortal Isobel.

Refusing to truly see her, he cut a swath, what humans would call a force field, to protect Isobel and the baby from any more bullets as she made her way to the gate of the abandoned churchyard and from there to the safety of the sanctuary door.

Then he turned his avenging might on the mur-dering mortals. Bullets lost their speed and trajectory and fell quite ridiculously to the ground. He would have been amused at the confusion of the gunmen had he any sense of humor remaining.

He transformed his essence so that he appeared in all his fearsome glory, with his white, powerful, feathery wings stretched wide. An aura of the most brilliant light surrounded him, and a terrible silence commanded the void.

Hovering above the fray, he awed the innocent and flooded the minds of the murderers with a terrible, roiling fear. His lightning bolts made their weapons so hot, their mortal flesh blistered. And when they ran away in terror, they ran straight toward cops descending upon the intersection from every direction.

At the end, Angelo used the heat to twist and warp the weapons so they could never again be used to take other lives.

And then, still from above her, he saw Isobel, still holding the baby, sink to the ground by the locked sanctuary door. Tears of relief streamed down her cheeks as she cradled the man-child close to her altogether human female form.

She knew her prayers had been answered, but not how. He knew that. She had seen him, but she was mortal now and would not have recognized him.

He could not avoid seeing her now, or recognizing her physical human being as the one he had known in every sense, save having bedded her.

He had ached then for the unfulfilled need of her. He ached now.

In his pure and angelic consciousness, Angelo wanted the earthly time back when he could have had Isobel in the manner of a mortal man. He wondered that he was not instantly banished from the ranks of angels, for lust and all the Seven Deadly Sins were forbidden.

His indiscretion didn't end there. He told himself

he only wanted her to see how reckless she had been, what danger she had been in, but in truth, he wanted her to know *he* had saved her life and the life of the baby. He wanted Isobel to know that without his intervention she and the babe would be dead.

He tried to excuse himself, to find justification for these ridiculously silly and trivial human longings. The fleeting desire might be forgiven; to act upon them he would be laughed out of the corps of Avenging Angels.

Most avengers knew what it was to deal in the real world with humans, even suffer attractions to them. But no mortal *needed* to know, as he wanted Isobel to know, who had come to her rescue, or why.

Lying, even to himself on such a private matter, was never an option for an angel. He knew better, as all angels must. He knew that he ached with his sensual, human memories of Isobel and of what they had been and done together half a millennium ago. He wanted to hold her in mortal arms, as a man.

He wanted to dry her tears. However noble the goal, his motives were not.

To go to her now, in that way, flew in the face of every value he had held for all his centuries as an Avenging Angel. Not the fact, but the power of his desire shocked him. He felt relentlessly drawn toward an action as dangerous as Isobel's plunging back into her mortal shape had been, as if he were being sucked into the vortex of a most immense and intimate hurricane.

He felt afire. Going to Isobel in any form was the last thing he must do.

He had driven off the attackers and made certain that in the confusion and disarray the police might search the grounds and look upon the exact spot where Isobel had concealed herself, but they would see and hear nothing of her or the babe.

Isobel was out of immediate danger. He could see to it that the murder of the baby's mother was avenged. He had duties, responsibilities, the charge of dozens of Avenging Angels in a city desperate for peace and justice. He could never forget those vast obligations.

Still he lingered, watching Isobel from a perspective unknown to her or any humans. She sat with her legs tucked under her in a flowing skirt that might, but for its immodest modern length, have served her well five centuries before. The baby's weight lay cradled in her lap, his head in the crook of her delicate arm. His wispy curls lay darkly against Isobel's porcelain-colored flesh. Her blood still flowed from her shoulder.

A human possessiveness took hold. Still, he delayed departing—as if rooted in place, though no such restrictions on him were even remotely possible.

He could not take his gaze from her.

In the same small-boned and voluptuous body that had been hers over five centuries before, Isobel stared into the little one's big brown eyes.

She hummed softly and, after a while, Angelo stumbled upon the terrible truth—the power of the emotion that had overcome Isobel's angel sense.

She'd been utterly transformed by the ancient magic of a mother's love for her child. He saw that in the primitive mortal brain stem she had taken in exchange for infinite consciousness, Isobel had already committed her love and her being to the babe.

She had claimed him for her own child in her woman's heart.

He saw that she would never willingly surrender her human form and give up the babe to his family or anyone else for any reason.

He found her utterly unfathomable.

Watching her stroke the babe's cheek, he also found her unimaginably beautiful. Her sable-colored hair spilled in gentle waves over her shoulders, her delicate features filled with emotion. Her eyes, like the silvery pools of moonlight on a glacial Alaskan river—the same silvery blue color that had once sent the great artist Michelangelo himself into raptures—shone with adoration for the babe.

And though her brave-heartedness in defying Heaven and Earth to rescue the babe touched him deeply, Angelo bent his will against her. He hardened his perceptions, refusing the excuses—what Grace would have called compassion.

He believed with all his being that what Isobel had done in forsaking her angelhood was not only unwarranted, and foolish, but worse, it was unforgivably selfish of her to take such risks.

He wanted to snatch her up by her beautiful neck and shake her. If it were within his power to make her resume her angel existence, he would have. What Isobel had done had never before, in Angelo's experience, been done within the ranks of the Guardian Angels; he knew that her act—in taking human form—was irrevocable.

He suspected she knew as well.

The consequences staggered even his imaginative powers. The babe was the target of some deadly human intent, some twisted passions Angelo knew instinctively had only just begun. And in her human form, Isobel could no more protect the babe or herself than she could fly.

Isobel Avedon might love the human child to the depths of her now mortal soul, but she was ill-equipped to keep him alive.

Angelo stanched the flow of her blood and departed from Isobel's presence. Deeply angered at her reckless choice, he knew all that was left to do was to seek dispensation for himself to protect Isobel's life, as well as the babe's.

For all his ruthless self-examination, he refused to question why he shouldn't give the assignment to another one of what the Avenging Angel Ezekiel had always called "the other halos."

Chapter Two

Seth finally cried himself to sleep.

Sitting deep in the shadows of the sanctuary entrance, Isobel rested her head against the carved wooden door. Her arms ached with the weight of Seth's small body, but it was a very long time before her mind began to examine the enormity of what she had done.

Flies droned by. In the sweltering heat of the day, sweat gathered between her breasts, at her nape, in the crook of her arm where Seth's head rested. Her sleeping limbs prickled beneath her. She hadn't thought to take his mother's purse, and she'd carried no diaper bag.

Isobel had no money, no clothes for herself, no change of swaddling for Seth—nothing. Worst of all, she had no earthly idea what she should do or where she should go.

She hadn't just fallen off any heavenly cabbage truck. She had heard tales of avenging angels conjuring whatever was needed to pull off a human façade.

She knew that in these cases, such accoutrements accompanied belief.

Ask, and ye shall receive.

She might have forsaken her calling in heaven, but Isobel *believed*. She bowed her head and asked for guidance. She asked for a place to go, a place no one would think to look for her and Seth. She asked for instruction on the way to get there, and then she asked for savvy to pull it all off.

The answering silence in her mind terrified her. Her heart pounded. She could hear the blood rushing past her ears, and she equated the sound with the panic flowing nearer and nearer her mind.

Dear God, what had she done?

How was she to protect this innocent babe when she couldn't even cope with leaving the shadows of the sanctuary?

A thousand times…ten times a thousand, she had rushed in to nudge assistance for women and children in trouble. She believed she knew every facet of the fear and isolation and despair felt by women throughout the ages in such straits.

It must have been true that she understood. How else could she have served her mortal charges in her role as Guardian Angel? But there was an immense gulf between the experience of Isobel the guardian and Isobel the woman. She had never been in such desperate circumstances herself. What would happen when those men came looking for her? For Seth?

Someone wanted the babe and his mother dead, and she couldn't accept on blind faith that no one else would come to end the sleeping child's life.

Pray, Isobel, she commanded herself. *Pray and move your feet.*

Seth stretched in his sleep, settling still closer to her side, and Isobel dashed away her tears. Love for the tiny boy swelled in her heart. Whatever else happened, she would not sit here wallowing in her fears. She had chosen this destiny, and she would take the very human responsibility that went along with what she had done.

Her legs had fallen asleep beneath her. She stood carefully, shocked by the prickling sensation she had forgotten. Shifting Seth's weight to her other arm, she knocked on the sanctuary door. It was a useless gesture. Had anyone been there, they would have at least checked outside the door when the gunfire began.

She breathed deeply and turned away. Following the overgrown path around the church to the street intersecting the one where the attackers had murdered Seth's mother, she considered what she must do.

Worn-out storefronts lined the opposite side of the four-lane street, but should she go there?

A bus? A cab? Seth whimpered in his sleep and scrubbed a tiny fist over his eyes and nose. He needed a more restful place than in her sweaty arms, she thought, as she stood on an unsavory corner of the barrio neighborhood. But she had nothing to give in exchange for a ride to a shelter for women and children.

She would simply have to walk. She screwed up her courage and crossed the street, then walked towards the closest storefront. All she needed was directions to such a shelter. Unfortunately, the shop she chose was the last one she would have picked had she had a dram of real-life experience. Or if she'd still had her angel's perspective.

A sign on the door read Shoe Repair Shop, so

when she spotted a woman through the window and then walked in, she was surprised to find that the place reeked of oddly pungent smoke.

Dread coiled around her heart. Saliva pooled in her mouth. The deal being negotiated on the countertop had nothing to do with shoes or repairs. She had never imagined herself walking so stupidly into the middle of such a transaction.

Either or both parties would have a gun, a weapon just as deadly at close range as the ones she'd only barely escaped by the grace of some heavenly intervention. How could she be so unwitting?

For the second time, Isobel wished she had the powers of an Avenging Angel, because this deal would hit the streets next, and then the veins of innocent kids too scared or angry or pressured to walk away.

She plastered what she hoped was a consummately ignorant and naive look on her face. Given the fact that she was standing here at all, naive didn't seem like much of a stretch. "I'm very...very sorry to interrupt. I'm looking for the nearest shelter for women and children."

The woman behind the counter straightened. Her lip curled unbecomingly. Her jaded eyes swept the small dirty store, then fixed on Isobel. "This place look like social services to you, honey?"

She wore a skintight black outfit that left her arms and most of her breasts bare. There were awful bruises on her upper arms. Isobel felt a flicker of recognition. This woman was someone she had watched over! Someone she had helped out of a scrape with a man who thought women were either for sex or punching out, depending on his mood.

Focusing only on the slight woman, Isobel willed her to remember the times when she'd needed an out quite desperately, and Isobel had been there for her, diverting angry blows.

"I know this isn't social services." Instinctively, Isobel held the woman's angry stare. "But you can help me, if you choose."

The woman looked torn, angry to be interrupted, scared that her buyer was getting antsy, yet still wanting to respond with whatever instinct was left in her to Isobel's appeal for help.

The moments stretched unbearably, until suddenly it no longer mattered. The unkempt, tattooed dope buyer swore and pulled a nasty-looking gun out of his leather jacket, jabbing it unsteadily in Isobel's direction. And worse, at Seth, who was somehow still sleeping against her shoulder.

"Stupid cow! You get it, lady? There's a deal goin' down here? Take a rocket scientist?" he snarled, spitting an ugly four-letter epithet at Isobel. "Get the hell outta here before I blow you 'way!"

Fear pounding through her, Isobel turned to protect Seth with her body and then bolted out the door, heading for the street corner as quickly as she could without jostling the baby awake.

Her heart wouldn't stop thudding painfully in her chest. She had been so close! If the woman had been alone, she might have helped.

But she hadn't been alone, and the deal she was involved in wasn't innocent; in fact, Isobel had been closer to no escape at all than to any real help.

Had she been an angel, she would have known what to do. Now, she had no clue, and she was terribly lucky the woman's antsy buyer was more interested in his next fix than in calling the cops down on his head for blowing her away with Seth in her arms.

If this was what she was to find in these run-down storefronts, she would be better off waiting until someone, anyone, turned up at the church. Approaching the corner, Isobel watched a child race ahead of a group of teenage boys to punch the button to cross the street.

She waited at the traffic light a few feet away from the teenagers eyeing her obscenely. She swallowed hard and straightened her spine, refusing to be intimidated.

Cradling Seth at her shoulder, she crossed the street back to where she had begun. The scarred sanctuary door, marked with graffiti she hadn't noticed before, brought home a sick, defeated feeling. Humbled—humiliated—so quickly, so easily, Isobel knew she would have to come up with a better plan.

She sank back down on the decaying adobe stoop and leaned against the rough plaster wall. Exhausted from his ordeal, sleeping longer, maybe, in his shock, Seth had gone without waking. He wouldn't make it much longer.

She rested her head on the door and prepared to wait, trying to imagine what she would have done if she still had the powers of a guardian angel.

She had been aided already. Someone, some angel, had driven off her attackers. She knew that because it was only by a miracle that she had escaped with Seth.

And somehow in all the confusion and hysteria, she had been left alone with little Seth. No one had come looking for her or the babe—not the police or paramedics—and that must have been an angel's touch too, leaving her time to comfort and ease the traumatized child into sleep.

But now she needed more help.

Now she needed the parish priest to return. With her angelic powers she might have found him and put the imperative into his mind—whether or not he had intended to drop by this afternoon or not.

In her very human fantasy of herself imagining her way out of this corner, the priest would know of a sanctuary where she might go to stay with Seth until she could get her bearings.

She needed a haven far from the church, a place so unlikely, so removed from this place where the murderers had shot down Seth's mother, that they would never find her. A nun's cell would do, or any homeless shelter, at least for a while.

She sat in a deeply shaded place, but the heat of the afternoon sapped her energy. She found herself struggling to stay awake—another human limitation she hadn't counted on. The toll which becoming human had taken on her was too great, and Isobel soon fell asleep.

When she woke, the midday heat had relented, but Seth was awake and fussing. Though his diaper was wet and heavy, through some miracle of modern science, the skin on his bottom felt dry.

But even if Seth wasn't physically uncomfortable, he was still crying, by now in a heartbreaking fashion. His tears wrenched at her heart. He didn't recognize her face, Isobel thought, or her scent or...her body.

Confused, his head turned demandingly toward her breasts, and his sweet bow lips made small sucking motions. His small, dimpled hand patted her impatiently, and the extraordinary sensation of her breasts readying themselves for the babe crept upon her.

If she had ever felt or imagined anything so startling or so exquisitely earthy or so sweetly sensual or rich, she didn't know when.

Awed at the miracle of her woman's body, she shifted to raise her clothing and offer herself to the hungry babe. He fussed a moment longer. Isobel felt to her core the babe's deep confusion, his hunger playing against the uncertainty. Isobel was not his mother, but her nipple tightened painfully all the same. After another moment, Seth latched hungrily onto her, and her pain became something else again, something profoundly pleasurable.

After a while, by instinct and wonder, she turned Seth and fed him from her other breast. When he had his fill, not a moment before, almost as if by a miracle of timing, the priest she had prayed for appeared before her.

A slightly built elderly man in a clerical collar and simple black clothing, he sank to his skinny haunches beside Isobel and Seth, who burped and stared unblinking at him. "I am Father Ramon Sifuentes, my dear. What have we here?"

Isobel breathed deeply, a sigh really. "Father. Thank God you're here."

He nodded, offering his finger to Seth to cling to. "When I was notified by the police of the shooting on the street, I hurried to the scene. They had already removed the dead woman before I could perform last rites, so I went to where they took her body." He hesitated. "Something told me I should stop by here..."

Her fellow guardians *had* been at work on her be-half, shepherding the pastor back to his small barrio church. "I'm very grateful. I need a place to stay, to take Seth and be safe. Do you know of a place where they will take us in for a while, some place away from here?"

Father Sifuentes's gentle brown eyes searched hers. His chin angled up. "You know the baby's name?"

"Seth."

"And he's your child?"

How to explain? Surely no answer was better than some made-up story.

"There was talk on the street about a baby caught in the middle of the shooting." His tone invited Iso-bel to confess that this child was not hers, but the dead woman's.

Why hadn't she thought of this? Realized she would have to answer to someone? Why hadn't she known that, of course, sitting here on the sanctuary steps, so close to the scene of the crime, anyone would realize that this child was the one who had fallen from his murdered mother's arms?

She didn't know how to lie. And it would be be-yond his ability to believe that she was a guardian angel come to earth to save Seth's life.

Seth gurgled and jabbered, grabbing a hank of Iso-bel's hair, wrapping it around his small fist. The priest's eyes never left hers. She swallowed hard, swallowed what felt like her human heart in her hu-man throat. "Like your coming here, Father, I came upon the babe because I was needed."

Father Sifuentes bowed his head, taking in what she had said, testing it against the instincts of a man who had served the best and the worst in his flock for generations. Isobel prayed he would leave it at that, let it go and simply help her to a place where she and Seth would be safe.

He had little reason to trust her. He had never seen her before, and even Isobel knew that there were women deranged enough with a need of a babe of their own that they would steal a newborn from his bassinet in the hospital. Would the priest think her such a desperate woman?

And isn't it half true, Isobel?

More than half?

She stroked the baby's plump thigh, and his sweet, dimpled elbow, containing his thrashing about in her lap. As much as she had wanted to save this beautiful child from the men who murdered his mother, she wanted more for herself than the prissy and pristine existence of a guardian angel.

She wanted to be a natural woman, a human mother. She had been cheated of that pleasure in her own time on earth, and she wanted her human existence now more than anything in heaven or on earth.

She wanted to gaze into wide, innocent eyes, to feel the tug of a baby's lips at her breast again, to soothe the tears and spend the decades it took to raise a male child to a man.

She wanted this babe so much, that she had willfully abandoned her duties and risked the wrath of the heavenly councils by plunging outside her element—and all because of a fleeting and dangerous and too-human maternal instinct.

She couldn't begin to explain these longings, or how she had simply materialized, not even to herself.

The mortal existence she craved was but the blink of an eye in all eternity. Surely it wasn't too much to ask?

Her very human panic must have shone in her eyes. The priest reached for her arm. "I think I must take you and the baby to the authorities."

"Give me a few days, Father," she begged him, cringing from his reach.

"What is your name?"

"Isobel. Isobel...Avedon," she added.

"What purpose will a few days serve, Isobel Avedon? So that you may fall more in love with a child that is not yours?"

"I could not be more in love with this babe, Father, but—"

The priest's eyes narrowed. "But?"

"I believe he is in grave danger from the men who murdered his mother. I only want to be certain that he does not become a target again. A few days. That's all I ask." *Dear Lord, how easily the lie came...* She wanted many more days.

"Are you saying, my child, that you believe the baby would not be safer in the protective custody of the authorities?"

"I don't know about that. What I believe is that *I* am meant to protect him."

Father Sifuentes squinted off into the distance, toward the western horizon and the setting sun and the gate where she had come into the churchyard. At last he drew a deep breath and shook his head. "You will not be safe in a shelter. There are those in such places who would turn you in to the authorities for another week of food and housing—or the money to return to the streets in search of booze or drugs."

Isobel nodded. She knew this to be true. "But—"

"May I suggest a bed-and-breakfast? There is one near San Juan Capistrano that belongs to a friend of mine, an elderly parishioner." His left eyebrow quirked upward. "Do you know the mission?"

Isobel smiled brilliantly. Know San Juan Capistrano? She knew it from long before the time that it was said that the swallows returned there each year. "I know it, Father. That would be wonderful."

Hope swelled in her heart. Even Seth gave the first precious, toothless little grin she had seen. There must be guardians in heaven looking out for her. "Can you take me there?"

He helped her to her feet, and led her to his serviceable old pickup truck. They stopped on the way at a department store. The priest paid for disposable diapers and a few small outfits for the baby, along with some sweaters and slacks and undergarments for her. Afterward he drove her to the century-old house on a bluff high above the aged Spanish mission.

The priest helped her settle into the small upstairs quarters his parishioner agreed to let. The main room displayed a rocking chair of some age, a view to the ocean from a window seat, and heavy twist-legged furniture adorned with authentic Victorian lace. Even the original heating system remained, and though Isobel jumped and cried out when the old steam pipes clanked, nothing could have dimmed her pleasure in the small rooms she had been given.

In the midst of taking his leave, the priest turned back to her, his eyes settling on the babe in her arms before returning to hers. "You speak of ensuring the child's well-being," he said. "I believe you."

"I intend only his well-being, Father. You may believe me."

He held her determined gaze. "Well enough. But soon, my dear, sooner rather than later, you must report to the authorities. Seth may have family already desperate for his return." His gently flowing Hispanic accent gave his pronouncement an added weight.

Isobel shifted Seth's weight to her hip. Was it possible that she could have abandoned her angel's essence for this baby only to find herself having to give him up? To be strapped with some overriding moral obligation to turn Seth over to his family, to another woman's care? Perhaps a grandmother or aunt who already loved him.

Her chin went up. "I'll make that decision when I know who killed his mother and why."

"You may never know that," he warned. "You must still reach his family and turn him over to their care." He held his hat in his hands. "Do you swear, Isobel, on your word of honor?"

She swallowed. Even though she knew that what she meant to do and what he meant for her to do were two different things, she said, "Yes."

Seth whimpered and jammed a small fist into his mouth, solemnly regarding the old man.

A shiver ran down Isobel's spine. A presence seemed to fill the high-ceilinged room. The old priest felt it too, Isobel was certain. His shoulders seemed to drop, as if released from tension, as if he had somehow been satisfied with her unsatisfactory answers.

As if, she thought, he had been reassured in some

other way, by some other being. Her uneasiness mounted.

She thanked the priest again for all his help and then closed the door behind him, determined not to worry, not to waste one precious moment with Seth.

She drew a bath and shared it with the babe, tended to her shoulder, dressed in a light cotton shift, then settled in the rocking chair to nurse Seth again. She rested her head back as the babe found her breast again and began to suckle noisily.

Pleasure almost too intense to endure cloaked her, body and soul. She stroked his sweet rounded cheek with her finger. But when she opened her eyes to gaze into Seth's, she looked—and then looked again—at the man sitting on a flowered chintz settee much too small for any man, but especially for a man his size.

"Angelo," she breathed, her heart thrumming as the babe nursed at her breast. "Angelo," she repeated in a disbelieving whisper.

"Isobel."

His voice resonated inside her, his eyes penetrated to her soul. Heat rose in her, making her flush, but whether from the heat of embarrassment or her attraction to Angelo, she didn't know.

Memories of his touch, of his kisses—memories now centuries old—flooded back to her. Powerfully built, virile, utterly pitiless, and exuding unending arrogance and strength, he commanded her attention. In every respect but one, he was the man she had loved centuries before, loved more than her own mortal life.

In that single aspect she found the cause of the

gnawing anxiety that possessed her. Angelo had looked upon what she had done, and she'd come up severely lacking in his fearsome judgment.

Chapter Three

Isobel cradled the baby closer. The heat in her body refused to abate. "Are you here to deliver your judgment, Angelo?"

"I am not your judge."

"Thank God of that."

"Iso," he began, then stopped, his voice, so nearly human, strained. "Why? Why, when there were so many options open to you?"

She broke off meeting his gaze, looking instead at the child for whom she had sacrificed everything she knew. Her own mortal life had been stolen from her before she could bear and raise children of her own.

How could she explain? How could she make him understand what incredible joy the babe had already brought her?

How his delight in splashing their bath water charmed her heart. How his fingers, poking into her mouth, touching her teeth, stole her very breath. How his sweet rounded tummy and curled-up toes begged her touch.

How his laughter made her cry and his tears broke her heart. He missed his own mother desperately, and Isobel had no doubt that the brutal imprint of her death would linger in his subconscious for a very long time.

"You know what was in my heart, Angelo. The babe's mother was murdered. He needs me. I still need what I could never have as an angel. It is as simple as that."

He shook his head slowly. His beautiful, brooding dark eyes held hers. "It is far from simple, Isobel, and you know it. As you said, the babe's mother was murdered. His own life is now very much at risk. How will you protect him? How will you find the men who murdered his mother?"

"The police—"

"The police have the gunmen, Iso," he told her softly, "not the ones who sent them in the first place."

She didn't trust the police or any authorities of the state, would never trust them even when another millennium had gone by. But...in so simple a matter? "The murderers will be forced to reveal who hired them and—"

"You will live happily ever after." Angelo stood and raked a hand through dark, wavy hair held back with a short leather thong.

His sarcasm was lost on her. Instead, the match of his exasperated gesture with her memories of Angelo de Medici stole her breath away. She had been a constant source of exasperation to him in their secret courtship, but then he had loved her to distraction for precisely that reason. He never knew what to expect from her.

Once, there had been another issue of great importance between them. The authorities had resolved the issue, in their jackbooted, blackhearted, murdering way. But this was different. Surely, in God's name, this was different.

"Do you think this can all end like some fairy tale, Iso?" he demanded.

"Iso*bel*," she corrected. Her temerity made it difficult to breathe. She didn't believe in fairy tales, or even, among the human race, the power of love, but she trusted that there was some reason—some higher purpose—operating here. Why else would she have even been allowed to abandon her angelic form, and given a human one suited to nursing an infant? "I am not your beloved Iso anymore," she went on. "That time, that existence was stolen from us. And for the mortal life of me, I cannot think why this must end badly."

"Of course not. Your intentions are always so good."

She stared at him. "And your pronouncements have always galled me!" she cried softly. "How can you be such a prig? Do you believe you are in sole possession of the truth? Are you the Lord's own arbiter of right and wrong, good and evil? Is it your judgment upon which He rests His own? How He must depend upon you!"

"Stop it, Iso!" The glow surrounding Angelo's powerful, masculine form quivered ominously. "Twice now you have acted on rash decisions, but my judgment is irrelevant. Had you the sense God gave a goose, you would know that you are in serious trouble, and for the sake of the babe, *for your mortal life*," he echoed her, pacing the room as if caged, "you had better figure it out."

Twice. *Twice now.*

She swallowed hard. Her throat seemed not to

work. Her human heart clapped like a kettledrum pounding a dirge. "Are you saying that you believe our deaths were my fault? That because I told my father... Angelo, *do* you blame me?"

He stopped, facing away from her. His broad angel's shoulders stiffened. "No."

Her chair ceased rocking. Seth fell asleep in her arms, and his lips released her nipple. Covering herself, she backhanded a tear. "Will you face me, Angelo, and say that you do not blame me?"

He only half turned toward her. "It doesn't matter, Iso."

She knew that he lied. He had no grievance toward her until the moment she had brazenly informed her father that she intended to marry Angelo de Medici. Any de Medici...

But that was ancient history. Here and now, he believed she had again done something so brazenly unfit: she had forsaken her place among the angels for the sake of an innocent child.

But an angel could not lie.

He *had* blamed their deaths on her rash decision to confront her father, yet in some way she couldn't comprehend, he had ceased to blame her. Otherwise, he could not justify denying that he held her responsible. She wanted very much to understand him.

"Angelo, please. It matters to me. Are you saying that you never blamed me, or that you have forgiven me?"

He sank down onto the settee as if the weight of all eternity had fallen on his shoulders. His gaze fell to the satisfied and slumbering babe, then caught upon the damp spot of milk that had seeped through her cotton shift.

He glanced quickly away and swallowed. The lurching thrust of his Adam's apple was as familiar to her as the stroke of a raven's wing. Scorched in some way by the intimacy of such a stain at her breast, he could not even control the telltale physical responses of the human image he'd conjured to present himself to her. A deep ravine of masculine insecurity had been exposed.

She knew he would retaliate. Being male, he simply wouldn't know what else to do. Angelo was about to come out with a truth she didn't know if she could stand.

It took him several more moments. "What happened," he said at last, "was not your fault, Iso. We knew the stakes. We knew the political fallout of our liaison—of our love. But if you had gone away with me instead of confronting your father, we would have had our lives together."

Her chin trembled. "I could not do that."

"Then it doesn't really matter what I believed then, or what I feel now, does it?"

Isobel straightened, symbolically adding to herself some small semblance of a backbone in the face of an outcome she had never imagined. Her emotions ran too high, too raw. Whatever consequences she might have expected when she made the fateful decision to plunge back into her mortal being, dealing with her past, with Angelo was not one of them.

It should not have mattered. They spoke of events and passions and political intrigues that had burned themselves out half a millennium ago. That it mattered so much threatened her in ways she could not name.

She rose and took the sleeping Seth to a bed made

up of a sofa turned the wrong way against the old plaster wall. Angelo's eyes followed her every move.

He had about his human form the aura of an angel. He had taken on a form she would recognize, but he remained a heavenly being. She well knew he realized to his core the primal satisfaction of the babe having nursed at her breast.

Without Seth in her arms she felt more vulnerable than ever. Angelo knew the scent of a palette of colors, the taste of a sonata. His keen angelic senses transcended ordinary sight, scent, touch, taste and sound. The synthesis of them gave him a commanding edge over her in any battle of wits or heart or intellect, and she could no longer bear to speak of their past with him.

Her only defense lay in seeking his help. "I know that there is someone out there who wants this little boy dead." She gestured awkwardly at the makeshift crib. "Was it you who drove away the murderers?"

He nodded.

"And you who brought the priest back to the parish?"

Again, he nodded. From the look in his eyes, she knew he had had a great deal to do with Father Sifuentes keeping her out of a shelter where she could be betrayed, despite the pastor's probing questions. Angelo, she knew, had placed those questions in the priest's mind.

His relief in dropping the subject of their past seemed palpable to her. He turned and waved a hand at the air, producing an immense black box against one wall of her primly Victorian room. The box immediately sprang to life, startling her with vivid images.

"These are the news accounts. You should understand what it is you've gotten yourself into."

She sank to the pillowed seat of a simple, wooden, black-lacquered chair beside a small tea table and watched as a woman's face filled an ephemeral screen. Isobel had never seen anything like it. A camel could well have gone through the eye of a needle more easily than she comprehended such modern contrivances.

The woman reporter began, "In the ongoing investigation of the drive-by shooting in this barrio neighborhood, KCBJ has learned that a baby was kidnapped in the wake of the murder. Authorities are speculating now that the shooting was both a means of disposing of the baby's mother and a cover for the kidnapping. Let's go live now to our reporter on the scene. John?"

Isobel's heart began to sink. Angelo conjured up a couple of glasses of a fine Sicilian wine and focused his attention on the screen as well, which showed an artificially lighted image of a man standing in the dark outside the church where Isobel had been.

The man began speaking into his microphone. "Sheila, what we know now is that there was indeed a baby who fell to the ground from the victim's arms. Several witnesses indicated that a woman seemed to appear—and I quote—'from out of nowhere.' This woman apparently snatched up the baby and ran. After that, the story gets sticky. While the shooters seemed to pursue the disappearing woman, even firing shots at her, she escaped cleanly, and no one thought to go after her.

"Detectives on the scene are apparently not buying into that escape. There were by preliminary counts at least fifty rounds fired, and only one bullet struck the fleeing woman. Witnesses indicated it must have been a superficial wound to the woman's shoulder or upper arm, since it did not fell her. Police are asking for any information leading to this wounded woman.''

When she checked, Isobel was stunned to find that her wound was suddenly healed, her flesh whole again.

Angelo had done it, had healed her. She would not be recognized by her wound, and she wanted to express some modicum of gratitude, but the story wasn't done and her attention went again to the television.

''At any rate,'' the reporter near the church was saying, ''the detectives have concluded that the shooting was carefully scripted. They believe the gunmen never intended to hit the mystery woman. If that is in fact the case, then the police fear the whole thing may have been a setup for a kidnap conspiracy.''

The screen image divided so the woman could now be seen as well. Isobel took a gulp of her wine. In her mind, authority *was* tyranny, police had a jack-booted mentality, and if they believed Seth had been stolen in a kidnap conspiracy, her point was made.

''John,'' the woman said, ''there are some pretty wild stories going around. Is it true that some witnesses insist it was an avenging angel who drove the gunmen away?''

''True story,'' he responded to the anchorwoman. ''That's what several witnesses claim.'' His lips curled in disdain for such apparently harebrained reports. "No accounting for eyewitness accounts, as they say. But in fact, the gunmen were taken to the emergency room of County General for third-degree burns to their hands—burns approximating the pattern of a handgun grip. The police aren't talking, though, and except for the consternation over the pattern of burns, the ER staff members whom I've been able to question are keeping this all under tight wraps."

Isobel shivered. "Make it stop. Please."

Without so much as a wave from Angelo this time, the picture and sound went still. "That was hours ago, Iso. There is more."

She ignored his warning and tried to focus on the facts, to concentrate on containing her paranoia. "I must have appeared to come from nowhere, but I don't understand the logic of assuming that I was conspiring with those murderers to kidnap Seth."

"They only know that you were not seriously injured by any of the shooting. Think, Iso. If you were them, you would have to consider what that means. They killed Seth's mother. How likely is it that if they really wanted to kill you and Seth, they would have failed?"

She felt herself chilling deep inside where the shivering didn't show. She knew, of course, that what the police and reporter refused to believe was true. It was only by the grace of Angelo's intervention that she and Seth had not been dropped dead to the ground exactly as his mother had been.

"It doesn't matter that there were eyewitnesses to your appearance, does it?"

Angelo laughed and shook his head. His commanding brow and strongly Roman nose dominated his profile, but when he faced her straight on, laughing, Isobel was struck by the pure masculine symmetry of his face, the mahogany brown of his eyes, the olive tones of his skin, the beauty of his straight, almost blindingly white teeth.

She resented his laughing at her. "It was a rhetorical question," she snapped. "I am not so naive as that."

He had never bothered stifling his endless amusement at her. "You are that naive, Isobel, and you have always been."

She jutted her chin. "And you have always been an ass about it." She hesitated. She wanted him to know she had not been some bubbleheaded sweet thing in charge of the cherubs for all these centuries. "A lot has happened since you knew me. I take the ugliness in mankind seriously now, whereas before I used to discount it. I admit that."

"And still you ask how they can believe you were in league with the murderers, Isobel," he chided. "You may never have had an ill-intentioned bone in your body, but that doesn't mean no one else does. And it doesn't mean they won't come after you with everything they've got."

"I didn't kidnap this babe," she uttered fiercely.

"I know you didn't." He hesitated and took her hand. She felt doubly scared. "So does the baby's father."

"His father?" If he had spent the ages calculating how best to destroy her, he could not have come up with anything stronger. She could barely get a sound past her throat. "His mother was unwed, and—"

"Iso, I told you there was more."

She pulled her hand away. She couldn't have Angelo's love. She'd been robbed of him, of that, too long ago to believe she would ever again have anything from him but the love any angel bears every mortal.

She didn't want his comfort or his pity, either. "Show me."

The picture on the large screen faded to black, and then Isobel watched as a different woman introduced a much older man sitting beside her. "In a stunning development concerning the apparent murder and kidnapping that occurred in the barrios this afternoon, we bring you tonight Mr. Ian James Candless, owner and CEO of Candless Industries, including the Rodeo Drive flagship store, IJ Candless & Sons. Sir?"

From her small stiff chair, clinging to an empty wine goblet, Isobel watched Ian Candless's aging, troubled features fill the screen. He had to be well into his sixties, but he had clearly had the advantage of the finest plastic surgeons and athletic trainers. Still, he looked straight into the living room at her, and his suffering seemed real to Isobel.

"I had thought to offer a reward," he began, "for the return of the baby kidnapped in the terrible drive-by shooting early this afternoon. My legal counsel advised that I couch such an offer as one made out of pure, charitable benevolence—a gesture to the community in which I have lived and made my fortune for fifty years.

"I could not do that. Until today, only my attorneys knew of the existence of my infant son, Seth, or of his mother, who was so brutally shot down this day. She was a beautiful woman with whom I shared a brief relationship more than a year ago. I never knew of Seth's existence until his mother tried, several days ago, to use our son to blackmail me. She expected that I would pay any amount to keep the living proof of our dalliance from Patrice, my wife of thirty-seven years, and my grown sons and daughter. She was mistaken. I regret the suffering of my family, but I could never shirk the responsibility of a child I fathered.

"Instead, through intermediaries, I established that the child is mine, and I offered this young woman a home on my estate in exchange for turning my son over to me. Neither I nor anyone connected with me saw her again until her photograph was shown on the early evening news as the murder victim."

Isobel felt her skin crawl. She couldn't point to anything Candless had said as being less than upstanding and honorable, yet she felt dragged through layer upon layer of slime. He had confessed to a "brief relationship" with Seth's mother, but in a tone and a context Isobel despised, as if his adultery were on a par with jaywalking.

"Men like Ian Candless never get their just deserts, do they?"

"They do, Isobel," Angelo assured her quietly. He had caused Candless's image and voice to freeze on the screen. "His soul is shriveled to dust. Ian Candless regards his grown sons as spoiled, ineffectual leeches not worth his spit. In Seth he sees a chance at a new beginning, a *tabula rasa*."

She stared at Angelo. "Do you *know* him?"

"We've met. Candless Industries have been subjected to a couple of IRS investigations and have come up clean each time. He frequents the Brentwood Smoking Club where Saint Michael and a few of the International Avenging Angels crowd hang out."

"Would I know them?"

"Rafe Santini?"

She shook her head.

Angelo gave a quirky smile. "You'd remember him. Women do. He deals in high-profile international crime."

She wondered fleetingly how he believed she would have crossed paths with Rafe Santini. More to the point, she wondered how well Angelo knew his own effect on mortal women, for he could not have failed to notice their appreciative gazes in his own age or any other. Or how enamored of him she still was. Even under these circumstances, the heat of her attraction pitted against the cold realities, knowing their chance had come and long since gone.

She caught herself up short. She couldn't dwell upon that. She needed to know more about Ian Candless.

"Do tales of adultery go over well in this smoking club?"

One of Angelo's heavy dark eyebrows rose. "Men do not label themselves adulterers, Iso. If you're asking whether Candless talked about his affairs with women, I don't know. I haven't been here very long."

"Can you find out?"

"Do you think it matters?"

"It matters to me what kind of man Seth's father is."

"If there had ever been any hint of a scandal before, Candless would have been quietly invited not to return. What matters," he went on gently, pointedly, "is what kind of father Ian Candless intends to be now, not his reputation in a Beverly Hills smoking club. And even now, he may be lauded for stepping up to his responsibility to Seth."

She didn't care what kind of father Candless intended to be, and Angelo knew it. She didn't have to point out to him that he had, in the last hour, called her on her own good intentions. "Is there more?"

"A couple of minutes."

She pulled her hair back and looped its weight in on itself to hold it back. "Go ahead."

"I have to warn you, Iso. Candless will show a police artist's rendering of you."

Her chill went deeper still. "Of me?"

He nodded. The picture flickered on. Candless's voice picked up. "The police suspect this young woman, whose face you now see on the screen, in the kidnapping of my son. I do not believe she meant to kidnap Seth. I believe she only intended to rescue him from the men who so brutally murdered his mother.

"I believe this woman to be a heroine. She risked her own life to save the life of an innocent child, and it's my opinion that she is, even now, hiding Seth away in the fear that his mother's murderers intend to kill my son as well.

"If you are out there watching now, young woman, let me say to you that I admire what you have done, and if you will only call, you and no one else, I will take my son, I will protect him against any threat, and I will reward you with whatever you ask. Please. This day you have proved yourself a heroine. Please. Return my son to me."

As soon as the newswoman took over to go to

reactions from the Los Angeles community, Angelo caused the television to turn off. In fact, to disappear.

Isobel made herself breathe. "Do you trust him?"

"I'm a long way from trusting Ian Candless, Iso. He's a past master at public relations, and a man who can and will say anything to get what he wants."

She nodded and rose from the small chair to walk off her chill. She went to the makeshift crib and looked at the baby sleeping soundly. "It's possible he's sincere. He knows I didn't kidnap the baby."

"On the contrary. He doesn't know anything about you. What he's done is make a brilliant preemptive move. He has managed to make himself sympathetic, and in the same stroke, he's said he will not pay a ransom. He didn't cave in to the mother's demands. He won't cave in for any kidnapper."

"He offered me a reward! I don't want it, of course, but—"

"But he didn't offer not to press charges, did he?"

"I don't know what you mean."

He smiled, a curve of his generous lips somewhere between indulgent and sad. "You would make a lousy detective, Iso."

"I would never dream of trying."

"In order to deal with your enemies, you have to think as they do. If you were to come forward and accept a reward—even if you didn't—it is still possible for Candless to pressure the DA's office to pursue kidnap charges."

Angelo had refilled her goblet. She longed for a healthy shot of the aged wine—for courage—but she declined. She had never looked to the dark, hidden agendas of others. If Candless's offer concealed such intentions, she needed Angelo's help more than she had imagined. "The babe's mother...her murder must demand your retribution."

"Isobel." He looked steadily at her, but his Adam's apple did a slow stroking descent again. He seemed more man than angel, more affected by her backward approach than he should have been. "Are you asking for my help?"

She straightened, willing herself to prove she had a backbone. "Yes."

"Then ask it." He stood. Though no closer to her than perhaps a few yards, his presence, his eyes on her, the focus of all his attention crowded her toward some nonexistent wall.

Her pride was at stake, but her mortal life, the life of the babe, meant more. "Help me. Please."

His human form, calculated to make mortal beings believe they were dealing with another mortal, breathed deeply.

"Will you do as I say?"

The sudden tension between them felt thick and throbbing as a pouring rain in a monsoon. Humor was the only defense left to her against such a question. "When did I ever do as you said, Angelo?"

"Never." He smiled again, and shook his head. "Will you at least trust me, Iso?"

Tears sprang to her eyes so fast she had no chance to hide them. She knew she had failed utterly to distract him from asking whatever he wanted. This question of her trust in him was a loaded one, and he knew it.

But perhaps she was making far more of this than it was worth.

She blinked away the sudden tears. "You're here with me to avenge the death of Seth's mother, and to safeguard our lives. I trust you absolutely to do those things.''

He must have understood the limits of her trust—clearly—because in the next instant, his mortal-seeming complexion darkened with anger. ''In the end, nothing may turn out as you would choose.''

''Is that a threat, Angelo?'' He had it in his power to thwart her attempts to remain with Seth.

''Of course not.''

She swallowed. She refused to let it lie. ''It feels like a threat. Like you're angry, like you will go out of your way to assure that I can never have what I want.''

He could not, it seemed to her, take his eyes from her face. Old passions lit his eyes, but his voice was without expression. ''Do you believe, Isobel Avedon, that I would ever do anything to hurt you?''

There it was again, the question of her trust in him, just phrased in another way.

''Answer me, Iso.''

''No, then!'' she cried. ''I do not believe you would willingly do anything to hurt me. But this child has no one who truly loves him. If Candless cared, he would have given Seth's mother anything in his power. I know that. So if you're asking me to accept on faith that things will not turn out as I want them, I cannot. Then you would be asking me to hand Seth over whether Candless's family will love and take care of him or not. That won't do, Angelo. I won't do it.''

Chapter Four

Angelo faced the toughest of all critics in his old friend Pascal. They'd agreed, in a manner mortals would deem telepathic, to meet at the Brentwood Smoking Club where men of Candless's ilk gathered for a fine cigar and espresso or brandy, perhaps a merlot as old as the hills.

Conversations here tended toward the sublime. No one got particularly disturbed over anything. What was the point of this fine establishment, if not to put the outside world at bay and bathe the senses in the exalted for a couple of hours?

But this night, the public revelations of Ian James Candless, carried on every California station and half the cable network news organizations, had the place in a mild uproar.

It was flatly unimaginable that the old man would claim an illegitimate son at this stage in his life. Why not pay off the mother, especially when you possessed a half-billion-dollar estate, and let your small indiscretions fade gently into oblivion?

Angelo thought it was a good thing Isobel was not here, or the good gentlemen of the Brentwood Smoking Club would have gotten an earful and more on the subject of "small indiscretions."

He couldn't blame her. She had spent hundreds of earth years in her guardian capacity easing the burdens of women left to cope alone with their babies, particularly the ones whose husbands—or at least the fathers of the babies—had left them.

A rose by any other name...philandering was still adultery, and Isobel had zero tolerance.

Pascal was amused. Not that he condoned such behavior. Lust was one of the Seven Deadlies, and adultery was specifically forbidden in the Ten Commandments. His attitude stemmed from Isobel's chronic naiveté.

"As long as human beings walk the planet, my friend," he said, pausing to fashion smoke rings that rose toward the ceiling, "sins are bound to be committed. Isobel is human again, bound to folly. What is your excuse?"

Angelo set aside his glass of wine. "I have none." He'd known their conversation would finally come to this.

Pascal's brow rose. "You will be asked to answer more fully than that before the heavenly councils."

"Don't you suppose that if I could come up with some mildly feasible explanation for my own intentions, I would practice it on you?"

Tapping ashes into a crystal ashtray beneath a small brass lamp on the table between them, Pascal backed off his goading. "What are your intentions, my friend? What is it that you want?"

Angelo bowed his head, blocking out the clink of ice in glasses, the scent of tobacco burning and the low murmur of masculine voices in the Brentwood Smoking Club.

In his mind's eye, he saw himself succumbing to the distant pull of his centuries-old attraction to Isobel. He saw her again, emerging from the bath she'd shared with the babe, her alabaster skin warm and flushed, her shift conforming to the curves of her body, her breasts swelled with milk for the child.

Isobel was alive again—truly alive—fresh and vital, bursting with life and a joy different from any an angel ever experienced. Her joy in being fully human was all the more precious for how fragile it was, how fleeting it might prove. Life was precious, and he found that he wanted it once more as well.

He shifted uncomfortably in the richly upholstered hunter-green leather chair.

Without so much as a word exchanged between them, Pascal nodded. He understood, better than any of their peers, the battle that raged in Angelo's consciousness between duty and desire, a desire he knew would never have arisen had Isobel not done what she had done.

Pascal had spent the better part of two hours laying waste to every argument Angelo could summon for taking on this case himself. He had given up. Angelo could lay waste to his own reasons, but only Isobel mattered.

"What will you do?"

"Help her, any way I can."

"Will you take on your human form?"

Angelo shrugged. "Whatever it takes." He offered his suggestions on a number of pending cases for the International Avenging Angels, then stood, struggling for a way to clarify, even to himself, what was at stake, why he could not hand over Isobel and the babe to any other halo.

"These things happen for a reason, Pascal. Surely there was divine intent that Isobel do what she has done."

Pascal blinked slowly, a wicked spark of humor lighting his eyes. "Ah, at last the old 'mind of God is unknowable' argument, is it? And by extension, surely it was meant to be that you and Isobel should meet again like this, else there is nothing but chaos in the universe?"

Angelo nodded and smiled, glad that Pascal understood.

"Mark my words, Angelo de Medici, you will make the choice yourself, to do exactly what Isobel has done."

"That will never happen. We were meant to meet again, in this way, I am sure of it. I want another mortal life to spend with her, but not now. I am an Avenging Angel, and I will always be."

Pascal shrugged, delighting in a physical essence with which to elaborate, and winked. "As we French say, *mon ami, Que sera, sera.*"

WHEN HE RETURNED to the small Victorian mansion set high up on the hill near San Juan Capistrano, Angelo found Isobel awake, curled up in the window seat, staring out into the moonlit night.

Materializing in his human-looking form, he stood well back in the moon shadows, curiously unprepared to speak to her. Her body was clearly silhouetted in the thin cotton shift. He found himself stirred in the most masculine ways, making him unable, as well as unprepared, to speak. Still he knew she was aware of his presence.

After a while, still watching clouds scuttle past the moon, Isobel broke the silence. "How did the police artist know what I looked like?"

Of such mundane things, he could speak. "Once the news broke, the pair of slugs you ran into at the shoe-repair shop fell all over themselves to get to the cops with your description."

"For money, then?" Her voice caught, frayed by the fear of an all-out search for her.

"Yes. A reward for information is a fairly standard thing."

"The same thing would have happened if I'd gone to a shelter, wouldn't it?" She refused to let the seeds of panic take root in her. "Someone would have betrayed me."

"Worse. You'd be in some eight-by-nine cell by now, and Seth would be in overnight foster care."

Isobel shivered. Her sigh was one of gratitude. Angelo found the last thing he wanted from Iso was her thanks. "What are you doing awake?"

"I couldn't sleep. I know my...that a body needs to sleep, but it makes me worry all the more."

"What does, Iso?"

That the police will come. "That something terrible will happen while I'm sleeping." Her head dipped low. Moonlight glinted off her sable hair like quicksilver. "That something will happen to the babe, or that I will awake and this will all have been a dream I dreamed out of season."

He saw clearly the genesis of her fears. Angels never slept, and so never dreamt. What need was there of dreams in paradise? But it was equally unheard-of that she had embarked on a mortal life again. She was afraid to waken and find that this was only some errant dream.

Fearful.

"It's only human, Iso."

She drew a deep, shuddering breath. "Something else I never expected."

"How could you?" Perhaps until this hour, she had herself forgotten her own powerful fear of men empowered to detain and interrogate any citizen, good and bad alike.

"I couldn't have remembered what real fear was like. You're right, as you have always been."

Her bittersweet remark caught him off guard, mostly because he knew it wasn't true that he had always been right.

She had already gone on to other things, other concerns. "I want to know the mother's story before I do anything about Candless's appeal to return Seth. I was wondering what she was doing in that neighborhood, and why she never contacted Candless again about his offer to let her live on his estate if she turned the baby over to him. How do we learn such things now that she's dead?"

"There are ways." He sat on the floor a few feet away from Isobel, his back against a wall. "You didn't know anything about her when the shooting started?"

"No. I had never been guardian to Seth before that time. How will we find out about her? About why she never told Candless she was pregnant with his child?"

Angelo looked curiously at her. "Iso, you know

that almost half of all babies born in this country are born to single mothers?''

She gave an impatient sigh. ''Better than you. I only meant that she must have had a reason for keeping her pregnancy a secret. Did she tell anyone? Did she have anyone to help her? Did she intend for him to ever know? Maybe she was afraid of Candless or what he would do. Maybe she knew he would kill her, or hire someone to do it for him. Maybe that's why she dropped out of sight again when he refused to give her any money.''

''Or maybe,'' Angelo warned softly, ''the babe's mother had only feared what you fear. That with all his resources and power, Candless would take the baby from her.''

Isobel's chin went up. ''Are you saying that with all his resources and power he would not have had to murder Seth's mother? If that's true, then why was she murdered? And why now, unless she represented a threat to him?''

''If she represented any kind of threat to him, Iso, all Candless had to do was to follow the legal advice he was given. He didn't have to admit to his infidelity or claim the baby at all to make the same offer after her death.''

Isobel pulled her knees to her chest and drew the cotton shift down to her ankles. If she knew what effect she created—how vulnerable, how feminine—she gave no indication of it at all. ''Do you think Candless is beyond caring what his family thinks? Why else would he make such a statement?''

''Maybe he intended to send his family a message.''

''Then he's using Seth's existence to bludgeon his

older children." Isobel shook her head. "Maybe I should just take Seth and get as far away from this city as I possibly can. He wouldn't come after me. He doesn't care enough about Seth one way or the other."

"I think you underestimate him, Iso. He has the clout to demand a police dragnet, and afterwards, to send private dicks after you for as long as it takes," he warned her, leaving aside the issue of how she would accomplish such an escape. "Is that the way you want to live?"

She didn't answer. He felt fear growing like a living thing inside her. Maybe he should have stopped.

"Iso, he controls a half-billion-dollar estate, and now he's publicly acknowledged that this baby is his child. At the very least, Seth is entitled to a share of Candless's estate. At the old man's discretion, Seth could wind up with the whole ball of wax. People kill for far less than what's at stake here." He glanced toward the makeshift crib. "They've already tried."

He didn't have to get any more graphic. He saw in Isobel's posture how clearly she understood the danger to Seth, and the threat he represented to anyone who stood to inherit a portion of the Candless estate.

"Will we even find anyone willing to talk to us about Seth's mother now?"

"There are ways." He approved her insight. It would have been far easier to find someone willing to talk before the murder of Seth's mother.

She turned expectantly toward him. "Can we...can you go back in time?"

Angelo went very still. Her suggestion blindsided

him, and he wasn't used to being taken by surprise. But he knew in the collision of his intellect and soul that if he were to go back in time and take Isobel with him, it would not be to investigate this murder.

He would take her where none of this had yet happened.

He would take her where they could live a mortal life together without impacting the rest of history, to a place and time where he could make her his, make love to her and have babies with her and grow old with her.

He could do none of those things. Not him.

Pascal was wrong.

It didn't matter how many times an Avenging Angel had returned to a mortal existence, or at least a mortal-looking life. In Denver, half his staff had sought such special dispensation. Sam, Dash, Kiel, tiny Ariel. He didn't begrudge them.

Nor would he follow them.

Isobel's eyes were impossibly dark in the shadows. Still he felt her gaze on him, and knew that her intuition was suggesting to her where his train of thought had led him. He felt her heat, her resistance, the thrumming beat of her heart; her certainty that their chance had been forever lost was cracking under the pressure of being together again in any form.

"It's not possible for us, Iso."

She shook her head, refusing to look at him now. "I only meant—"

"I know what you meant," he interrupted harshly, "but when this is done, when the murder of Seth's mother has been avenged, then, Iso, I will have to...I will have to go. There are still more evil acts to avenge than there are stars in the galaxy."

Her head dipped low again, struggling with deep emotions too old to conquer. "You misunderstood me, my heart. I chose my fate, to be a mother to this child. I have not pinned my mortal heart on such an impossibility as your joining me."

"Isobel—"

"No. No more. Please. Tell me how we can find someone who will talk to us about Seth's mother."

He could sit no longer, watching her, knowing her heart—knowing she had done the forbidden for a purpose that had nothing at all to do with him. He got to his feet and began to pace the confines of the long, narrow sitting room.

He felt constrained, caged. Trapped in a never-never world of lost possibilities. It battered his faith to know it was his own desires and not hers that he must conquer.

"Angelo?" He turned from matters of faith to deal with her question, but she had her own idea. "If the police gave a reward to those two in the shoe-repair shop for my description, couldn't we offer a reward? The tabloids do it all the time, don't they? Put out word on the street that you'll pay for information?"

"That's a fine idea, Iso—"

"Maybe you could just shove the offer back in time by a few days. That way we wouldn't have to wait."

He smiled at her. The suggestion was worthy of an experienced Avenging Angel. "There's hope for that chronic innocence of yours."

"There has to be. I'm responsible for this baby now."

Angelo nodded. This was what Isobel wanted, what she had traded for heaven. "You know, even word on the street will alter the way this all plays out?''

Isobel straightened, for in that instant she knew that their strategy would shove Ian James Candless's back to the wall. With word out of an illegitimate heir to the Candless fortune, he would have no choice but to either deny Seth altogether or acknowledge him as his son.

They already knew what choice he would make. What they couldn't know was whether he would have made the honorable choice if his hand hadn't been forced.

THUS IT WAS that word hit the streets, nearly seventy-two hours before the murder of Seth's mother, of an outrageous offer for information on the illegitimate son of Ian James Candless. Angelo put out a cellular phone number that could not be tracked or located, and an answering mechanism to screen the crank calls.

Isobel sat listening to the calls with Angelo for a couple of hours the next morning. Most were useless. At least seventeen women called claiming that Candless was the father of their child. Any one of the claims might have been true, and Isobel's mood soured with each one of them. If even a fraction of those calls had any merit, Candless was a worse excuse for a man than she had imagined.

The thirty-seventh message had begun to play when Isobel walked away to get a fresh diaper for Seth. His toothless grin reeled her in, and in a moment she wasn't even really hearing the woman's voice leaving the message.

Angelo stopped the message to replay it, and she

was vaguely aware that the messages had stopped playing, but she was busy playing peekaboo from behind the baby's diaper.

"This is it, Iso. This is the one."

Reluctantly, she shifted her attention to Angelo. "Are you sure?"

He nodded. "Listen."

I have the information you want, but I won't go public. The sultry voice gave only a phone number where the woman could be reached, no name or address.

Isobel taped the diaper into place and gently pulled Seth into a sitting position. "Should we call her?"

"I'd rather see her in person. It won't be a problem to get her address."

It wasn't. With one telephone call to amenable authorities, Angelo knew her name was Kathryn Weston, and that she lived in an upscale townhouse in a Beverly Hills subdivision. Angelo materialized a jet-black BMW to create the image of someone with the bucks to pay for the kind of information they were seeking.

Which didn't even address the real problem—that Isobel and Seth might be recognized—or the even stickier problem of why some high roller willing to part with a small fortune for whatever information the woman might have would be going around with a woman and a baby in the first place.

Isobel wasn't going to be content to leave the investigation to Angelo, and she wasn't going anywhere without Seth. She wouldn't have given the first consideration to leaving him in the hands of Mother Teresa herself.

Angelo wasn't going anywhere without Isobel, ei-

ther. The standoff demanded a resolution. He was
used to traveling alone, acting spontaneously, without giving thought to a woman and child.

"Isobel, I can cloak you and Seth so that no one
will recognize you as the woman in the police sketch.
What I can't do is to make it a reasonable proposition
that any woman with an infant would be involved in
going after some sleazy tabloid tale."

"Then don't try," she answered sweetly, standing
on the porch of the Victorian house, shading her eyes
against the noonday sun. "Let the woman think what
she will. If she wants the money, she'll talk."

Angelo gave it up and closed the door behind him.
In another minute they were all safely belted into the
BMW headed north on the Pacific Coast Highway.
Traffic was light, and Angelo opened it up to speeds
the state wouldn't approve.

Inside forty minutes he pulled to the curb on a side
street intersecting the one where Kathryn Weston
lived. He knew, in the way an Avenging Angel just
knows, without physically inspecting the three-
thousand-square-foot townhouse, that Weston was at
home and alone.

He helped Isobel from the car, lifted the baby from
his car seat, then placed Seth in her arms. Together
they approached the row of houses beneath palm
trees and canopies of bougainvillea.

Kathryn Weston answered the door in chic, silk
paisley pajama bottoms and a blazing orange-silk
halter top. Deeply tanned, her long, bleached blond
hair spilling over her shoulders, she wore multicarat
diamonds on every other finger.

She wasn't pleased to find strangers at her door.

Isobel got the impression that Kathryn had been expecting a man—probably a very wealthy one.

Angelo turned on the charisma. "Kathryn?"

She angled her chin, eyeing Isobel, radiating haughtiness. "Who are you?"

"Angelo de Medici. This is my wife, Isobel, and my son, David." He clearly lost vast ground with her by introducing a wife, but, on the other hand, she relaxed a little, obviously feeling less threatened. "You called about information on the illegitimate son of Ian Candless."

Beneath her tan, Kathryn Weston paled. "How did you find me?"

"It doesn't matter."

"It matters to me," she snapped. "I left a phone number. I have nothing to say to you."

"I think you do, Kathryn," he persisted. His hand rested lightly on the small of Isobel's back, but his focus, his whole demeanor focused on the other woman. "You said you have pertinent information."

"That was before. I have nothing to say to you—or anyone else."

She tried to shut the heavy oak door, but in some unseen way, Angelo thwarted her efforts. "Before the child's mother was murdered, you mean?"

"Yes. Before that. I've no wish to get myself murdered, Mr. de Medici, so again, I have nothing to say." She gave him a speculative, seductive look that totally dismissed Isobel's existence. "Come back another time, when you aren't so...occupied."

Shielding Seth, Isobel wanted to scratch her eyes out. "Maybe you would rather tell your story to the police?"

"Don't you dare threaten me with the police," she

hissed. "I won't have it." Again she tried to slam the door shut, and again she failed.

"Kathryn." Angelo tilted his head forward. His voice insinuated an intimacy Isobel had only heard centuries before, and only with her. "Talk to me. Tell us about Seth's mother. I promise you no trouble will come to you because of it."

Whether it was his eyes or his promise or his voice, Isobel didn't know, but after a long silence, Kathryn Weston took a step back and let them in.

She turned on her heels and led the way across a foyer of painted and glazed terra-cotta tiles to a sunroom furnished in white wicker, an extravagant floral print and antique bronze candlesticks.

She sat on a chaise longue. Angelo took the larger of the wicker chairs. Isobel settled at his side on an oversized footstool. Sucking on his pacifier, Seth lay in her lap, his eyes following the slow turn of a white ceiling fan. Isobel was acutely aware of Angelo's now divided attention, his uncanny, angelic ability to focus his attention in two places at once.

He sat there in that white wicker chair, too masculine to bear, too intensely, darkly handsome for even Kathryn Weston to ignore, taking in every detail of the woman's behavior, and at the same time, watching Seth, cradled in the skirt between Isobel's thighs.

In some devastatingly sudden and uninvited and untimely way, desire for her flared in his eyes. It could have lasted only an instant, but the heat of it burned in Isobel until her lungs ached for air.

"Angelo."

His name came out in a whisper, a plea to stop and a plea to go forward, a plea to douse the flames between them, because where it would lead was an impossible place, out of space and time or the grace of any miracle.

He broke off looking at her, his face a mask of forced indifference. If Kathryn Weston had noticed the brief exchange, Angelo relieved her of the impression. She looked with distaste at Seth. "Gina's kid is about that size."

Isobel stroked the curve of Seth's head. "You've seen Gina and her baby recently then?"

"Not since she told me her plan to get some, uh...*generous*...child support from Ian Candless."

"Then, to your knowledge, he is the father of Gina's baby?"

Kathryn plucked a cigarette from a gold case on the glass table before her and lit it. "He said as much last night on television." She exhaled sharply. "Surely you didn't need me to confirm that."

Isobel tried to focus on the interview, but she couldn't help feeling bereft since Angelo hadn't looked toward her or the baby again. She knew now that she had to make him stop seeing her that way, making her see him the same way. It would break her mortal heart to fall for him, to allow her feelings for him to come roaring back after all these centuries.

She hadn't come back to a mortal existence for that. He had to understand.

She had no choice, sitting in Kathryn Weston's extravagant sunroom, but to smother her feelings, bury her trembling hands in Seth's blanket and listen to Angelo deflecting the woman's animosity.

He began with questions that wouldn't provoke Kathryn's defenses. Questions meant to uncover

Gina's side of the story so Isobel would know how to respond to Candless's televised plea.

"How long did you know Gina?"

"Altogether, less than two years."

"Go on."

"Since she came to L.A., all right? There isn't much to know. She arrived on a bus from Utah, fresh and dewy and stupid. She went to a couple of talent agencies. One of them hooked her up with me." Her choice of words and inflection pretty well revealed exactly the relationship she had had with Gina Sellers. Kathryn Weston ran an escort service, and young, inexperienced girls were quite a find.

Angelo looked at his hands. His gentle tone reminded Isobel of a hypnotist, able to assuage any fear. "Did she know what she was getting into?"

"Not at first. But Gina was desperate. She'd followed some jerk here who had promised her the moon and then dumped her. I took her in, got her some decent clothes and within a couple of weeks, I arranged an introduction between her and Ian Candless."

Isobel felt a slow burn begin inside her. "Couldn't you have sent her home to her family, Kathryn?"

She laughed. "Some of us don't have that option. We do what we have to do."

"And that includes setting up desperate girls with men like Candless?"

Her eyes glittered with disdain, and her tone was icy. "Please. Don't presume to judge what you can't possibly understand."

"I do understand—"

"I doubt that very much." Kathryn snapped. Her expression grew rigid and angry, dismissing Isobel as a fool. "Gina was one of the lucky ones. Candless was her first—and her last, and then she quit."

"One of the lucky ones?" Isobel repeated. Her throat ached. Kathryn Weston had learned only one way to respond to the conditions in her life, and that way was the only one she had to offer Gina Sellers. But in the end, it had cost Gina her life. "She's dead, Kathryn."

The other woman shrugged. The grisliness of it made her too flippant. "It happens."

"Do you have any idea who would have wanted to kill her?"

"Who are you people?" she shrilled. "What do you care? I thought you wanted information about an illegitimate Candless heir for some article, not—"

"We do," Angelo interrupted. "We still do."

"Yeah, well, you sound like cops, and I have nothing to say to you."

"We're not cops, Kathryn," Angelo swore to her, meeting her brittle edge, compelling her with his eyes and his tone to back off her attitude. Isobel swallowed hard, retreating inside herself. She had let her emotions get in the way of getting the information they needed.

"The existence of an illegitimate Candless heir was always an explosive possibility," Angelo said, and again trained his eyes on her. Isobel knew Kathryn had forgotten, due to the sheer magnetism of his countenance, that she had meant to say nothing more.

"Now that the baby has been taken and his mother murdered, the story is even hotter," he said, but Kathryn only dragged on her cigarette and stubbed it out. He went on without a trace of reproach. "Do you know who needed Gina Sellers dead?"

"Other than Candless's grown children, you mean?"

"Anyone less obvious, yes."

"His wife. His son-in-law. His business associates. His public relations firm. His lawyers. Rumor had it that there were illegal immigrants employed in the clothing factories he owns."

Isobel took the baby's tiny exploring fingers from her mouth. "Did Gina know that?"

"She told me the last time I saw her that he had gotten some kind of phone call. He was on a speakerphone and didn't know she was around. She said there were some officials making noises about inspecting his employment records. When he saw that she had overheard him, he gave her this heartwarming song and dance about providing a better life for the underprivileged among us."

"Like the people who live in the barrio where Gina was murdered?" Isobel guessed. This might explain Gina's having been in that unsafe neighborhood in the first place.

"I suppose."

"Do you know why she told you about this?"

"I don't know. To warm my heart?" Kathryn laughed unpleasantly. "I don't think she believed him, but I doubt she knew what to believe. A part of her had to know Candless uses people."

Isobel gave a troubled sigh. "Would knowing any of this give her leverage for blackmailing Candless?"

Kathryn shook her head, doubtful and disbelieving. "Maybe, but she didn't know anything firsthand. Why would she do that anyway, when she had his son? Wasn't that blackmail enough?"

"Apparently not," Angelo said. "Not if Candless was prepared to preempt the threat of exposure by telling his family and the public anyway."

"Maybe she did resort to that, then. I couldn't tell you. I know she meant to get the money out of him, but I never saw her again."

The baby had grown restless. Isobel shifted him into a sitting position. "Why else would she have been in that neighborhood, though? Did she live there?"

"No."

"Here with you, then?"

"She lived in a condo six or seven blocks away." Kathryn recited an address. "She had a one-year lease, prepaid. It was up this month."

"Then," Angelo concluded, "their relationship wasn't as brief as Candless claimed."

"A couple of weekends." She laughed harshly again. "No more. However brief, living arrangements were a typical parting gift from him. Cheap, by his standards, and ever so compassionate."

Isobel rattled a chain of plastic keys to distract Seth from his growing fussiness. "Before the baby was born, did Gina ever try to tell Candless she was pregnant?"

"It wouldn't have done any good for her to try. Ian Candless is surrounded by people whose job it is to make sure he isn't troubled with petty details."

Angelo posed one last question, mostly, Isobel thought, to prevent her from lashing out on the subject of men like Ian Candless and petty details. "Do you believe he was really prepared to let her live on his estate in exchange for handing over his son?"

"Why don't you ask him?"

"I'm asking you."

"Better yet," she challenged, ignoring the demand, "ask his son."

"His *son?*" Isobel blurted out in dismay.

Her elegant eyebrows rose. "Bruce always did his daddy's dirty work." She gave one last, dismissive shrug. "Collecting Ian's mistress, and dealing with her afterward, fell into that category."

Chapter Five

The provocative option of going directly or somehow indirectly to Bruce Candless, to follow up on Kathryn's allegation, appealed to Angelo. If he'd been alone in this, he'd have gone for it. But there was a lot to be said for checking out Gina Sellers's condo as well, and they were already in the neighborhood.

They made the short drive from Kathryn Weston's condo with the purpose of finding out what they could about Gina's life and intentions in her last weeks. But from the moment Angelo tripped the lock and opened the door of the condo, Seth began to whimper. At some level he recognized the place, familiar colors and textures and scents, and in his tiny heart, he expected his mother to be there.

He didn't understand, and though he had been fussing to be fed, he refused to nurse, struggling instead to be free even of Isobel's arms.

Sitting on the elegant chintz-covered sofa in the house Ian Candless had provided for Gina, Isobel fought to stay calm herself. The babe was inconsolable. Had she still had access to her angel powers, she would have been able to ease his uncomprehending heart.

She had never felt so helpless or inept. She tried everything, while Angelo scoured the condo for any stray piece of paper or envelope, or notes scribbled in the margins of the telephone book. He checked every drawer and cabinet, every nook and cranny.

Neither of them was successful. Not the smallest hint remained of the people Gina Sellers might have spoken to or even known. At the ragged edges of her awareness, Isobel knew Angelo had concluded that someone had beaten them here, but she was consumed with worry for the baby.

Nothing she did for him seemed to comfort him. He was only five months old, but he was grieving for what he couldn't even understand. His mommy, the face he knew, the only caretaker he had ever known, wasn't here or coming back.

"Iso, it's not you," Angelo offered at last, desperate, she thought, to help salvage her crumbling composure. "Let me take him."

She nodded and allowed him to take the babe, to do for Seth what she would have done if she still had her guardian powers. In the space of a heartbeat, the babe fell asleep, his anguish eased. Angelo laid him down on a thick, downy quilt at the end of the sofa.

Isobel had only just stood to walk off her tension when a sharp rap came at the door.

"Open up! This is the Immigration and Naturalization Service, Agents Terrence and Landau. Open the door now and stand back!"

Isobel froze. Her breasts already ached, heavy with the milk Seth had refused. Now dread coursed through her body. They would surely take Seth away from her, or hand her over to the ones who would.

Her heart hammered. Her mortal body began to sweat. She doubled over with the pain in her chest.

"Iso, what is it?" Angelo demanded sharply.

"The police," she whispered in their native Italian, the term she used conveying *black-hearted bullies*—fascists in another time. Her slight body, even her voice trembled. "Don't let them take him. Dear God, don't let them."

"Isobel," he commanded, giving her shoulders a jarring shake. "Isobel, stop. Think. Deal with this. You are strong enough, you *are*. These are not thugs and they're not after Seth."

But he saw from the fear in her wide beautiful, haunted eyes that Isobel was caught up in memories so visceral she couldn't breathe, much less think clearly. In a trice he acted to create a warp that left the agents outside Gina Sellers's condo virtually frozen in time, and then he cupped Isobel's stricken face in his big hand, using the connection between them to join his mind to hers.

What he saw in the images of her mind shook him deeply.

He saw himself turning from her, from their kiss, startled by some unexpected noise in a courtyard of a fifteenth-century villa. The air was thick with the scent of jasmine, the moment rife with emotions unspent between them.

But in moonlight, in the eerie silence of her memory, he saw the glint of a sword arcing toward him, slowly, deliberately, inescapably now, delivering a killing blow to the side of his head with the blunt side of the weapon.

The clash of flesh and bone and blade dropped him to his knees. He saw himself fight to get back up, stumble and fall again to the ground. He had never stood a chance, and the only way that was possible was if he had been betrayed.

Isobel's awareness flared in her memory for all too brief a moment, encompassing the image of her father forcibly dragging her across the cobbled stones, away from the grisly scene and her beloved's fallen body. He watched her fight her father tooth and nail, lose her wrap and her slippers and her dignity before her wrist snapped in her father's grip.

All the fury and wrath at his disposal in his role as an Avenging angel rose up inside him, fury with nowhere to go. Isobel's courage and fire and passion for him had delivered her to this, but the worst was yet to come. His attacker came out of the shadows, and in the man's face, Angelo had his first taste of her raw and unreasoning panic in a condo in Beverly Hills five centuries later.

Never before had he seen the face of his murderer, or learned his identity. Now he knew he was the captain of the guard, a man in the employ of the prince to whom Angelo was allied, and allied with his enemies as well.

The face belonged to Vittorio de Medici, Angelo's own brother. At his murdering back stood an easy half-dozen others, men under his command who were sworn to guard Angelo's life, and Isobel's, with their own.

The distant, fearsome rage gripped him. In her memory her broken bones meant less than nothing. To him the betrayal by the untrustworthy guards, even by his own flesh and blood, meant less than the harm that had befallen her. But Isobel feared them all for the blackguards they were, for the way they used and abused their power, for the way they could be bought and sold, twisting and distorting the truth until even murder could be justified in their minds.

"Isobel."

In an instant, he made the decision to materialize into his truly human form. There was always a toll— a price to be paid, a loss of certain powers, the sacrifice of objectivity. But his spectral form was without warmth or real substance, and unless he made that change, he could offer her no real comfort.

When his transformation was complete, he took her into the shelter of his arms, surrounding her with his physical body and his warmth. He could not take from her the horror of her memories.

He could not erase her fear, or even make it manageable.

It was not outside his powers, even in his human body, to confer those consolations, and in truth, it was exactly what he had done for Seth. But Isobel must cope in the world she had chosen, and he would do nothing that would finally strip Isobel of her own resources.

"Angelo." She went naturally to him, clinging to his shoulders, resting her head against his warm and solidly male chest. For the first time in five hundred years, she could smell his skin, feel his heat, hear his heart beat. Memories of her long-ago lover collided with the very real man before her and drove everything else from her mind.

Her throat tightened. This was the flesh-and-blood, imperfect man she had once loved more than life.

This was the man whose mind and scruples and soul she admired above all others.

This was the man whose secret glance stole her

breath, whose arrogance and swagger and judgment galled her...and whose touch she craved.

She raised her head. Her eyes came to rest on the cleft in his chin, on the pits and pores in his skin, the evidence of a dark and heavy beard shaved close.

Pleasure too intensely human threatened to swamp her. The crush of her heavy-laden breasts against him incited her toward him; he was rigid and aroused against her belly as well. But she knew his temporal form, his humanity, his *humanness* was only an elaborate illusion.

His lips caressed her brow. Tears more sweet than bitter spilled from her eyes. In that fleeting, ethereal instant, she would gladly have died for it to have been her lips he kissed. In the end, she would be left again to do without Angelo.

She had to remember that it was not for Angelo but for Seth's sake—and the maternal longing inside her—that she had defied heaven and hell.

What was it to her, after that, to pull her human self together and defy the men at the door, or Ian Candless himself?

She stepped back, brushing the tears from her cheeks, and took a deep, steadying breath. She forced a certain fearlessness to appear in her eyes as she met Angelo's gaze. A careful scrutiny of his eyes revealed feelings for her she knew to be as deep as her own. "Will you let them in now?"

He nodded slowly. "If you're ready."

"I am."

"Remember they are only men, Iso." His eyes glittered. His voice cracked lower. "And remember what you have done just now."

She swallowed hard. His regard for her strength in

backing away from the comfort and protection of his arms awed her. "I'll remember." She breathed sharply, then breathed again for courage. "Shall I...will they recognize me as the woman in the artist's sketch?"

His gaze had never left hers. He could continue to cloak her appearance or not. Though fully human now, his extraordinary powers remained intact, unlike Isobel who had forfeited everything to become human. Only avenging angels were spared their powers. "It's your call."

She straightened, nodding, not trusting her voice to sound as if she weren't really certain. "Then do it. Drop the cloaking."

Approval radiated in his smile. He cuffed her gently on the chin, then strode to the fireplace. He had chosen, she understood, to put himself behind her and let her deal with the federal agents as she must. He rested an arm on the stone mantelpiece, and at his nod the knock came again.

Isobel looked to the sleeping baby to assure herself they had not awakened him, and then went to open the door.

The agents stood waiting, impatience carved in their expressions. The one closest to her, fortyish and overweight, his pug nose flaring unbecomingly, had been reaching behind his body and beneath his suit coat for a gun. The other, taller and more pleasant-looking, already had his weapon drawn.

Shaking inside, Isobel demanded they put away their guns before she would move aside. "There is no need of weapons here. I won't have them drawn around my child. Please keep your voices down as well."

The pair exchanged glances and put away their handguns, too slowly to suit her. She moved aside. The heavier one introduced himself as Agent Marvin Terrence. "This is Agent Clive Landau." They moved past her into the condo, and Seth was, of course, the first thing that drew their attention.

She looked to Angelo. She thought his presence would have commanded their attention first.

"They believe you are alone, Iso," he warned her.

"Is this the Candless kidnap?" Terrence spoke almost at the same moment as Angelo, so she knew they could neither see nor hear him.

Shivering, uncertain, she nodded her understanding to him and then looked directly at Terrence and his partner. "The Candless *baby,* you mean?" she retorted coolly. "I believe he is, yes. And I am the one who saved him."

Landau glared at her. "That hardly makes him your child, ma'am."

She refused to rise to an accusation that mocked her and insulted her intelligence in the same breath. "He's in my care. What is it that you want?"

"For starters, your name. What you do. What you're doing with this baby."

"Isobel," she said. "Avedon. "I'm a guardian...sort of. A nanny."

Again the two men exchanged glances. Terrence began to work his way around the living room, looking for something, anything—whatever men like him looked for. Or maybe he meant to unnerve her, to keep moving while his partner grilled her.

"A nanny," Landau repeated. "Don't nannies usually take the baby home at night?" he demanded, bearing out her intuition.

"Nannies," she returned coldly, "aren't usually witnesses to the murder of a child's mother."

"Oh, I see. You're afraid you're targeted." He obviously didn't believe her, as contempt for such a lame excuse at ducking kidnap charges thickened his voice. "Why haven't you turned the kid over to Candless?"

She glanced at Angelo and gave a shrug. "I don't intend to 'turn the kid over' to anyone."

Terrence's head jerked sharply around. "You're not interested in Candless's offer?" he demanded.

"No." Both of them waited for her to elaborate or justify, somehow explain herself. She wouldn't start, but she could see that she was only making them angry and despite her resolve, she needed Angelo's measure of these men.

Angelo responded to her as if she had spoken her musings aloud. "They didn't come here looking for Seth, Iso. It's dumb luck on their part and they know it."

"Listen," she said finally, taking her cue from Angelo's counsel. "I was there when the baby's mother was murdered. I only wanted to save his life, because whoever did this obviously meant for him to die, too. You had no idea when you came here that you would find me or this baby. For all I know, you're the reason Gina Sellers was murdered."

Landau shot his partner a guilty, telling look. "What do you know about it?"

"Nothing," she returned, piqued by the barest flush of anger on the agent's narrow face. "What is there to know? What did Gina have to do with you?"

Angelo grimaced. The agents were under no ob-

ligation to reveal their purposes. He leaned—hard—
on their consciences till both men cracked.

"Look." Landau sighed heavily, his brow creased
in aggravation. He looked to Terrence, and at the
other agent's slow nod, he continued, "Gina Sellers
had agreed to work for us, to get onto the Candless
estate and act as an informant in a sort of Trojan-
horse operation." He gestured with his head toward
Seth. "She had the perfect entry. Ian Candless
wanted his son. He offered Sellers a home. All she
had to do was go along with his proposal."

"I don't understand. What are you after? How
could a young, frightened, inexperienced woman like
Gina be of any help to you just because she lived on
Candless's estate?"

Landau coughed. The sound made Isobel's skin
crawl. "Exactly. Gina Sellers was young and inexperienced, and on top of it, she had nowhere to go.
Her lease here was up. She needed money. She'd
grown used to this sweet deal, and she wasn't prepared to hit the streets again."

Isobel shook her head, not fully comprehending.
Gina might have been desperate enough to go along
with their plan, but what was the point of *anyone*
getting into Candless's estate if it was his business
practices that had come under investigation?

"There are any number of possibilities, Iso," Angelo responded softly, as if she'd verbalized her
question. He moved behind the agents so she could
see him as he spoke. Creating a temporal space in
which Landau and Terrence would not recognize the
passage of any time, he explained. "Candless could
have removed business records to the estate.

"He—or his sons for that matter—could be conducting illegal operations from there. Gina was a long shot, but a perfect opportunity—and it sounds like they'd run out of options.''

Isobel nodded. The logic sickened her, the willingness to use Seth to get his mother onto the estate of criminals. ''Why would she have agreed to do this just to bring Candless down? How would that serve her interests in the long run? If Candless had gone to jail, she might have wound up with nothing.''

Angelo shrugged. ''Humans don't often think past the ends of their noses, Iso. If she wanted revenge, and the Feds promised her that, with her help, the old man would live out his life in a prison cell…then, why not?''

''I don't get it, Angelo. We have to assume she wanted revenge on Ian Candless, or else she was in desperate need of money.'' Isobel understood Gina's desire for revenge, if that's what it was, even for money. What she couldn't imagine or condone was a woman agreeing to anything at all that would put her baby at risk, or into the hands of evil men as some sort of pawn, even—or especially—if one of those evil men was her baby's father.

She watched Seth sleeping beside her for a moment, then straightened. ''What is this investigation about?''

Terrence gave up prowling, sat in the club chair matching Landau's and took over explaining. ''Illegal immigrants. We've been trying since the beginning of the year to nail Candless—or his sons—on counts ranging from blackmail and extortion to facilitating illegal immigration for cheap labor in the company's clothing factories.

''Our investigation into the business practices of

IJ Candless & Sons is at a standstill. We need eyes and ears inside that estate. We could go after the staff, but it might take months to accomplish. Gina Sellers could have gotten around that immediately.''

Isobel felt an eerie, awful anxiety taking hold of her heart. ''And you're telling me all of this because…?''

''You have the kid,'' Landau stated, bald as that.

''Excuse me?''

Glowering at his partner, Terrence's jaw tightened. He tried to take a less offensive route, to smooth it over with her. ''Ms. Avedon, listen very carefully. If we chose, we could toss you in the slammer and throw away the key. We could take the baby. We'd rather salvage the operation. You have essentially the same offer from Candless now that he made to Sellers. He thinks you're some kind of heroine, and he knows what you look like from the police artist sketches. You could, if you choose, simply replace Sellers in our plan.''

In a heartbeat her anxiety turned to anger. ''Your scheme can't possibly work now!'' she cried. ''They know, or someone knew, exactly what you were up to, and that's why those men shot and killed her. *You're* responsible for Gina Sellers's murder!''

Terrence stretched his neck uncomfortably. ''It's one possibility.''

''Among dozens, I'm sure,'' Isobel snapped. ''How do you even dare ask me to put myself and this baby into such a position?''

''Two reasons, Ms. Avedon,'' Terrence said. ''One is that it is highly improbable that anyone would suspect you. You have no prior connections to Candless—in essence, no one has anything to fear from you. Sellers was a different story. She had not only given birth to an illegitimate Candless heir, she was your archetypal 'woman scorned.' She had an ax to grind. As far as she was concerned, Candless was going to suffer. You have nothing against Ian Candless, and if I've understood you, no desire for any reward whatsoever. He may wonder how any woman could interrupt her life in such a manner. We have to hope you can pull it off. Make him believe you had no real life before in any case."

She hadn't, of course, but Terrence was very wrong to believe she had nothing against Seth's father. He was every bit as responsible for Gina Sellers's death as these men. But she was waiting to see the other shoe drop. "What's the other reason?"

They should have been clued into her resistance by her tone, but if they were, they didn't care. "Frankly, Ms. Avedon," Landau said, "you don't have much of a choice. We have no choice. Candless expects a woman with your appearance. There are active kidnap charges and warrants out for your arrest. There is a natural parent waiting to take custody of his child. You won't see this baby or the light of day again for thirty years...unless you cooperate fully with the ongoing investigation."

Isobel swallowed hard and looked to Angelo. "Can you lock them out?"

"Lock who out?" Landau asked, but in another instant he was silent, his brow frozen in a puzzled expression.

She got up carefully from the sofa so that she wouldn't disturb Seth, but then she began to pace. Angelo watched her, keeping his silence.

"I already know what you're going to say."

"Do you, Iso?" he asked gently.

"Yes. This is, of course, the perfect opportunity for me to see what kind of man Candless is. Maybe they're wrong, you'll say. Maybe their investigation stalled because there is nothing there to find. Maybe, you'll say, I'll find that he is a changed man who has found his scruples again. Or, if what these immigration agents believe is true, and if I help them, then Candless really will go away to prison, and I will get the legal guardianship of his baby son. And isn't that what I want, finally?"

"Isn't it?" he asked, admitting by his smile that she had covered the possibilities he would have suggested. There were others. Gina Sellers's murder to avenge. The hundreds of lives affected if Candless was exploiting illegal laborers. But he wanted for her what she had sacrificed so much to have. "Isn't that exactly what you want, to have Seth to raise as your own?"

"Yes. But Angelo, it is not as simple as that! It's easy for them," she waved in the agents' direction, "to say that no one will suspect me of taking Gina's place, but what if someone does? I'm supposed to just take it on faith that I won't end up dead? And if I die, what happens to Seth then?"

"Iso, you don't have to take it on faith. You will not die, nor will Seth. I promise you that. But faith would not hurt you. That's the human condition, that you cannot know how things will turn out. Forget their bullying tactics!" he urged. "You know I will not allow you to spend your mortal life in prison. And Terrence is right. You have no choice. Isobel, you know it yourself. *This* is the day you have to stare down every naysayer, even the one inside yourself. And if that means going along with a plan that offends your sensibilities because that's what you have to do, then you do it.''

She swallowed as hot emotions pooled in her throat. "It's not my sensibilities I worry about, Angelo.''

"I know. But I have promised you no harm will come to Seth, so it is only your sensibilities left.''

The flicker of doubt in her wide silvery-gray eyes slammed into him. He was asking her one more time to trust that his promises to her were good. That she could depend on them with her life—and Seth's—when a matter of only an hour ago, he had seen in her memories what little good his temporal promises had been to her.

"Iso—''

She stopped him. "Don't say it, Angelo. Please. I have only one choice, it's true, but it is my choice, and I will not even ask for your promise.''

She would not ask, but in all heaven and earth, he swore, no harm would come to baby Seth...or to Isobel Avedon.

Chapter Six

At midnight, he left her sitting before the upstairs fireplace in the old Victorian house on the cliffs above San Juan Capistrano, nursing the babe at her breast. In the morning she would make the call to Ian Candless, committing herself, body and soul, to the path she had chosen when she took on her human existence again.

He thought, as he roamed the heavens in search of peace in his soul, that he would not make it. That Pascal was right. That he would, in the end, defy the heavenly councils, forsake his role and return to earth, to Isobel.

The clash of duty and desire had never been so stark.

He could not take issue with his own decision to transform himself into his mortal being in the hour of Isobel's greatest need, but the cost to his equilibrium staggered him. He had not expected or prepared himself for the onslaught of human sensations, mortal feelings, and the desires of a human male in the presence of the woman he loves.

His physical body had betrayed him, and were it not for Isobel's strength in turning back from the brink herself, he would have denied himself nothing of the pleasures of finally making love to Isobel Avedon. The immigration agents could have stood motionless and unwitting on the porch of Gina Sellers's condo until dawn, for all he cared.

How Pascal would laugh to learn the truth. The great and mighty Angelo de Medici—principled, arrogant and honorable Avenging Angel—born a virgin, had died one as well, for he had only ever had eyes for Isobel, and he would not bed her until the day she became his wife.

He had counted himself a master in the art of postponing his gratification. Character, he told himself, was forged in such fires as he had gone through denying himself the service of her body. He knew of no one else—including the priests of his acquaintance—who had never once indulged the pleasures of the flesh. Angelo de Medici was different, above the rest, special.

And a total, monumental, epic fool.

He would not have been taken off guard on that night in Isobel's memory had he had any instincts about him but the rutting sort. When he was with her, he could think only of her, and that had proved to be his downfall.

He was empowered differently now, even when he took human form. If he chose, he could make the world go still for as long as it took to finally make love to her. In his mind, that would more truly join them through all eternity than any vows before any mortal official.

And Angelo de Medici did not take vows lightly.

So he could not even tell himself that he must back away from his desire for Isobel in order to keep his wits about him, to protect her. His wits as an angel were always about him, and the threat of any danger could be countered in any split second—even supposing he forgot to stop the world while he made love to Isobel.

He wanted her. There could be no danger. To make love to her would in both their minds be to unite them inextricably through all the ages. They had served heaven's purposes a thousand years between them. Surely in God's eyes they were entitled one night together.

He would settle for one night.

All that kept him from her was Isobel herself...that and the knowledge that he wouldn't be able to bring himself to settle for only one night.

ANGELO CARRIED the two suitcases and diaper bag to the BMW parked below. Isobel watched him from the window in her second-story room, where sunlight streamed through the aging windows, casting prisms of wavering light.

She held Seth close to her shoulder, his head tucked beneath her chin, her finger tucked in the sweet little folds at his neck. His baby smell mesmerized her heart. She could not remember such deep content as in these moments when his tiny fingers and gurgling noises and sweet smell crowded everything else from her mind.

In an hour, maybe less, she would make the call to Ian Candless. Already she felt trapped, like a sparkling dust mote caught in the sunlight, carried on currents not of her choice. This was the part of being human she knew all too well but had forgotten in the chaotic moment before choosing to become human again to save Seth's life.

But if she had it to do over again, she would make the same choice. The baby gave her this comfort and joy. The world quickly swallowed up the simple pleasures. Mortals took them too much for granted. Isobel resolved to try in every single moment to savor the sweet and learn from the bitter.

And then there was Angelo, whose dark hair shone like the coat of a mink in the sunlight below, whose human physique made her mortal mouth water, who had held her during her crisis with the immigration agents. Dear, sweet Angelo had let her go, despite his obvious desire, to deal with those agents and her life herself.

Her heart thumped just watching him clean the windows of the car with a chamois and spray he had carelessly conjured out of nowhere. Yesterday in Kathryn Weston's sunroom, she had wanted to take him on. To have it out. To make him stop wanting her. To make him realize she could not possibly fall in love with him all over again, only to have to live through losing him again.

Standing there in the window, holding Seth to her shoulder, Isobel finally understood what rubbish that was. How could she fall in love with him all over again, when what she felt for him had never lessened?

So Isobel finally admitted to herself that her heart would not break to lose him back to the Avenging Angels. She would survive because that was what she chose. But, just once before he left, she wanted him for her lover.

She turned briskly away from the window and put

Seth into his infant seat, tickling his tummy, smiling for him, cooing and making baby talk while she buckled him in and tears spilled onto her cheeks.

She might as well wish the sun would rise in the west and set in the east. Angelo would never so forsake his honor as an Avenging Angel.

IT HAD TAKEN the combined efforts of three federal law enforcement agencies to prepare her, virtually overnight, for their Trojan-horse operation.

In the suitcases Angelo loaded into the BMW were half a dozen skirts and blouses, several pairs of slacks and jeans, sweaters, a sweat suit, clothes for Seth, and a cellular phone in case of dire emergency.

In addition to Landau and Terrence, a couple of men from the FBI and a woman INS agent, Carolyn Mapes, came to deal with the incredible opportunity that had dropped into their collective lap. Because of the artist rendering, Isobel was the only woman on earth with the leverage Gina Sellers had had in getting into the Candless estate.

Isobel had been instructed for hours yesterday afternoon in the art of behaving as if she had no interest in the Candless household, except for Seth.

That wouldn't be a problem for her. Seth *was* all she cared about. Still, she worried. "Candless will have to agree to hire me as Seth's nanny first."

Candless was on record calling Isobel a heroine, and he could not very well turn around and demand she be arrested for the kidnap. But all four of the men had been tempted to discount any possibility that Candless would refuse. After all, he'd offered the woman who'd saved his baby any reward she desired. But Carolyn Mapes, whom Isobel had liked at first sight, agreed with her that this might be difficult.

"He probably will try to put you off," Carolyn said. "He'll be expecting to part with money, not to take a stranger into his house. Maybe he'll take to it more easily if you just ask for a couple of weeks to prove yourself."

She'd laughed then. A pretty, dark-haired woman with a few extra pounds and a generous smile, Mapes had three kids of her own. "Trust me on this, Isobel. Candless will have his suspicions. There will be serious questions. Obstacles. But you have nothing to hide. Let him ask. Let him doubt. He will find you to be exactly what you are. Besides, when that household sees what it is to deal with a five-month-old, they won't want you to go."

"I wouldn't," Angelo had put in, his eyes fixed on her. "Want you to go, that is." Invisible to the agents, he'd been keeping up a running commentary. She couldn't stop herself from looking up into his dark eyes. To the agents she must have appeared to be daydreaming.

Carolyn reached across the space between them to touch Isobel's icy hands. "Are you okay? You look a little...flushed."

She had had to force her attention back from Angelo. "I'm fine, really. I just don't understand my role, you know? If I'm to be the baby's nanny, why would anyone in that house say anything around me that could be useful to you?"

Carolyn nodded, but she was watching Isobel more closely. "This is the thing, Isobel. We believe that there is always going to be a falling out when people get greedy and start breaking the law. Some get more greedy and want to crowd their luck, and some just want to stay on the safe side. Or they don't believe after a while that the division of the spoils is fair anymore. They get nervous, tempers start to flare, and," she shrugged, "under pressure, they start dividing into camps. They begin grumbling and plotting against each other. The story's as old as Cain and Abel."

Angelo was staring off into space now. In some way she couldn't explain, she knew he was reminded of their own history. She knew that despite the vast amounts of information available to him as an Avenging Angel, he had never known before what he saw in her memory—that it had been his own brother who had struck the blow that took him from her. Family, one pitted against another, as old as the sons of Adam and Eve.

"Anyway." Carolyn sat back, apparently satisfied that Isobel was okay. "We're interested in what goes on in the Candless family. Our investigation may have stalled, but if they're like everyone else, they're feeling the pressure."

Isobel nodded. "And now, Ian Candless wants to bring his illegitimate son home to his family."

"Exactly." Carolyn grew more earnest. "Additionally, someone murdered Gina Sellers, and it's not a far reach to suggest her continued existence, and Seth's, was a powerful motive to any of the legitimate heirs."

Isobel nodded. The murder investigation would continue. Carolyn Mapes made it clear that no one involved was discounting the murder.

"It's a pressure-cooker situation, Isobel, and we desperately need you to be our eyes and ears. Whatever alliances you can manage to strike up among the staff will be useful, because the hired help inevitably sees a lot of what's going on. In short, we are looking for ways to exploit even the smallest fractures in family loyalties.''

Other agents came and went in discreet clusters at the small Victorian mansion. She was provided with several dozen listening devices smaller than the backs of pierced earrings, powerful enough to pick up both sides of telephone conversations, virtually undetectable by conventional sweeping methods. She had only to leave one behind wherever she could.

Although Angelo agreed with the underlying logic, that Isobel's and Seth's presence in the Candless stronghold would drive up the stakes, he thought the state-of-the-art bugging contrivances primitive and hokey. They would doubtless work in their haphazard way, but their value was entirely dependent on Isobel's gaining access to places a nanny was unlikely to be welcomed, or even allowed.

No. It was well within Angelo's powers to open the entire estate, every private encounter, every telephone call, to a single multichannel recording device, for his own purposes and theirs, and that's what he intended to do.

The agents promised to be listening to every bug at all times. If she needed advice or help, if she needed out fast, she had a set of key phrases to alert the agents who would be on the listening end.

Now, facing the moment in which she must enact the Trojan-horse operation in Gina's stead, Isobel left the baby in his infant seat to go wash her face. She hadn't been crying, yet her eyes felt swollen. Splashing cold water on her face felt like a very powerful metaphor for what she was about to enter into. A dip in the ocean might be even better. Like it or not, she was now in the thick of a criminal investigation, when all she had wanted was to love one motherless little boy.

She swept the cold droplets from her face and stood up. She knew Angelo was behind her, even though there was no reflection in the mirror over the sink pedestal. His image would not reflect. Another reminder to her of the way things were—it was the one reality check she really didn't need.

"Are you ready, Iso?" he asked.

Patting her face with a hand towel, she nodded. "Almost."

"I'll carry Seth down to the car. Take your time." He turned away.

"Angelo—"

"Iso?" He turned back.

"I..." She broke off. What had she been going to say? She didn't know. She wanted some reassurance, maybe, where none was possible. "Thank you."

She thought he knew instinctively that there was much more she couldn't put into words. He only answered in kind. "You're welcome."

SHE SAT on a cement bench in a sliver of a park on Dana Point above a marina near Laguna Niguel watching the yachts and gulls. Angelo had taken Seth with him to a spot more than a hundred yards away near a small playground. Isobel couldn't see them, which meant Candless couldn't either. But Angelo could see her, and he would bring the baby when she gave the sign. She would only wave when she had satisfied herself that Candless had come alone, and they had struck a bargain.

Exactly on time, and alone, wearing ordinary jeans, a light blue polo shirt and a baseball cap, Ian Candless approached her bench. He moved without any of the infirmities of old age. She thought the television cameras had done little to convey his vitality. Or perhaps he'd regained it when she called.

"Ms. Avedon?"

She nodded. "Yes. Isobel."

He offered his hand. She gave him hers. He seemed choked up. "Where is my son?"

She screwed up her courage. Everything depended upon gaining his respect. "Nearby. I hope you don't mind. I wanted to meet you first."

He shoved a hand through his full, snowy white hair. "You'll have to excuse me, Ms. Avedon. I'm anxious, naturally, to finally see for myself my new little son."

Isobel wanted intensely to dislike him. He was, at the very least, a philandering husband, and if the federal crime strike agents were to be believed, much worse, exploiting human labor. But in person and outside those realms, he could not have seemed more genuine or been less demanding.

"Seth is a wonderful, special baby," she agreed, "but he's had a very hard time of it."

"Of course. Terrible, terrible how Gina died, holding him in her arms." Candless asked if he might join her on the bench, then sat when she agreed, careful not to crowd her in any way. Squinting against the sun, he swallowed. "I regret very much what happened to her."

"She didn't deserve to die."

"No. No one does. Not that way."

His words seemed genuine enough, but she wanted badly to abandon everything else and ask him straight out if he had had anything to do with Gina's death. Would he be so genuine then, so sympathetic? No. She needed to be discreet now, and let the charade play out. If Candless had ordered Gina's murder, he would pay. She had to believe that.

"I've handled this poorly," he admitted. "I wish I had done better. I wish, frankly, that Gina had come to me sooner."

"You're a very formidable man, Mr. Candless, and well-insulated from…distractions. Problems. Do you know for sure that Gina never tried to come to you?"

"It's possible, I suppose, that whatever attempts Gina might have made could have been stonewalled by well-meaning employees."

"I don't think they could have been well-meaning, sir, and still have turned Gina away. Not by any definition I know."

He stared a moment at his hands, which, more than any other part of his appearance, disclosed his age. "You are daringly honest, Ms. Avedon. I'll say that for you." He looked closely at her. "But I may not be quite the cad you undoubtedly believe me to be."

"Do you feel you must have my good opinion?"

"You wanted my measure, isn't that right? You wanted to know what kind of man you are turning Seth over to?"

"That's true."

Nodding, he went on. "I hope to be judged, Ms. Avedon, not by what I have done, but for what I am willing to do and be for Seth. I hope, perhaps, to

make it up to Gina by giving our son a good life."
He looked at Isobel. "Tell me, how can I thank you
for what you have done in saving Seth's life? What
reward would you like? What dream—"

"I don't want any reward, Mr. Candless." And it
was not in his powers to fulfill her dreams.

"Surely there is something you need, something
you want. Please. Name your price."

"I have nothing, Mr. Candless, so I want nothing.
I have no family, no ties, no friends within a thousand miles, no one except Seth. What I want is to
stay with him."

Candless frowned. "Stay with him?"

"Yes. He needs me. You must have need of a
nanny—"

"I'm afraid that's all been arranged. I've already
hired a very competent woman who came to me
highly recommended."

"But if you're asking what I want, Mr. Candless,
as a reward for saving your son's life, then I'm telling you, that is what I want."

"I can't just dispense with the woman—"

"I think," Isobel interrupted softly, "that you are
a man who can do anything he wishes to do. Give
whatever financial reward you were prepared to
make to me to the woman you hired, to compensate
her, and let me stay with Seth instead."

"Are you serious?"

"Quite serious, Mr. Candless. I want this position.
I think Seth has already been through enough, don't
you? This is not a good time for him to have to get
used to still another caretaker."

His frown deepened. "Have you a résumé, Ms.
Avedon? Credentials?"

Isobel met his look straight on. "I saved your son, Mr. Candless, and I kept him from harm. He is used to me. He trusts me. I've eased his nightmares and dried his tears. What other credentials would you like?"

He gave her a rueful look. "You're taking advantage of an old man, young lady."

"I want this very badly."

"Well, you certainly make a powerful case for yourself."

She pressed her advantage. "Then you agree?"

He laughed. "Do you know when was the last time anyone handled me so efficiently?"

She didn't know what to say. "Nineteen-fifty-seven?"

He chuckled again. "Well before you were born, let's put it that way. Where did you get such *ovarios?*"

Isobel laughed out loud, but she would not be charmed out of her request. "I've taken care of hund...dozens of babies, Mr. Candless. I've never fallen for one like I fell for Seth. He's a charmer, too, even at five months. Please. Will you give me chance? A month to prove myself?"

Candless breathed deeply and stood. "Show me my son, Ms. Avedon, and you will have your chance."

HIS MEETING WITH SETH went poorly. Angelo, appearing in the guise of the priest who had first helped Isobel, came at her wave, carrying Seth. Isobel introduced him as Father Ramon Sifuentes. Meeting Isobel's eyes in a dark and shadowed look she didn't understand, not even acknowledging her success, he handed the baby over to Candless.

Seth began immediately to fuss and squirm. Candless was scarcely more comfortable himself. He hadn't a clue how to hold a baby. He grimaced in keen disappointment, adding a helpless smile. "I suppose my expectation of an immediate bond with my son was a bit…unreasonable. Ms. Avedon, would you help me, please?"

Isobel nodded and took Seth from him.

Angelo smiled humorlessly at Candless's attempt at self-deprecating charm. "The baby isn't all that happy anywhere outside Isobel's arms, Señor Candless, I can assure you."

She buried her concern about Angelo's dark mood in the baby's neck. What he had said wasn't, strictly speaking, a lie, but neither was it too near the truth. Seth could lie for hours in Angelo's hands, contented, communicating in a sacred, special sort of way humans rarely achieve between themselves.

Shading the truth, implying Seth was only truly happy in her arms, protected Candless from disappointment. She might have been amused at how adept Angelo was at skirting an out-and-out lie, but his demeanor as the priest wasn't exactly warm.

"Am I to understand that you've agreed," he said in the priest's sonorous Hispanic tones, "to allow Isobel to be the child's nanny?"

"I have." He gave her a considered look. "She's a very persuasive young lady. And my son has certainly taken to her."

"I would like very much to stay in contact with Isobel," Angelo said. "Would you allow me to visit her?"

"She will perhaps prefer," Candless countered smoothly, "to have some time off once each week. I would not object to her visiting with you. Do you feel you must keep tabs on me, Father Sifuentes, or on Isobel?"

Angelo shrugged as if this was not the case at all. "The Lord keeps tabs, *señor*. As for me, I would only like to hear of this young man's progress in the world," he answered, cupping Seth's head in a sort of blessing.

The baby smiled and reached out a hand to touch his father's face. The old man melted, exactly, Isobel guessed, as Angelo had wished him to do.

Meeting Candless's chauffeur with Isobel's luggage in hand to preclude any questions as to why a barrio cleric would be driving a BMW, Angelo assisted with the transfer, then took Isobel's hands, offered a blessing and turned away. Candless offered Isobel a hand in, then slid comfortably into the seat opposite her. After the limo turned the corner, Angelo dematerialized as Father Ramon, then appeared at her side in the limousine so that only Isobel could see him.

THE FRONT GATE was a formidable combination of form and function. No one gained access to the estate without the gatekeeper's direct action. Angelo guessed the approved list was a short one.

Spectacular mountain vistas surrounded the estate, but it was set upon grounds so completely flat for miles around, that it would have been impossible for crime-force agents to stake it out, set up or conceal state-of-the-art directional listening equipment, or even approach with less than a minimum of ten minutes' notice to the Candless staff. The gardens were landscaped in desert style to within a hundred yards of the house, and an impregnable stone fence began at that point and circumscribed the residences.

Angelo counted four such structures—the main two-story residence, with wings stretching out from a central building, two guest houses and one that appeared to be a much smaller echo of the main house. Candless pointed from one to the next.

"My second son, Conrad, lives in the closest guest house with his wife, Michele. The one at the far end is occupied by my daughter, Kelsey, and her husband, Emory St. John, who is chief counsel for IJ Candless. They're expecting my first grandchild at Christmastime. My other sons, Bruce and Harrison, live in separate wings of the main residence, and that one," he pointed to the smallest outbuilding, "is divided into several small apartments for staff."

At last the limousine pulled into the circle drive of the enormous main house. The drive was cobbled and exquisite, lined with gracious, extravagant bushes and vast numbers of flowers and flowering cacti. The house itself was done in authentic stucco, with clay roof tiles; the architecture would have compared favorably with international five-star resorts.

The chauffeur, Halpern, opened the door and helped Isobel out. Candless followed. The front door opened and a beautiful golden retriever puppy bounded out, barreling for the car.

Candless laughed delightedly, bending low and clapping his hands for the puppy, who wriggled and jumped and barked uproariously. "Brandy, girl! See here, Ms. Avedon, my son Seth's first dog. What do you think of her?"

"What a pretty puppy! See the puppy, Seth?" She turned the baby so he would see the dog, but the five-month-old was more startled than enchanted by the barking. Isobel smiled. "She's wonderful, of course. Brandy is her name, did you say?" Kneeling with the pup between his legs, Candless crooned her name. "I think you'll have to give Seth a couple of months, frankly."

He glanced up at her. Seth had not started to cry, but the puppy hadn't held his attention either. "I suppose he is a bit young, but... What can I say? I want my son to have the best of everything, right from the start."

"That shouldn't be a problem," Angelo commented laconically, leaning invisibly against the roof of the limousine, one booted ankle crossed over the other.

"Will you stop?" Isobel demanded, crooning to the baby as if his chewing her finger—and not Angelo's running commentary—was what she meant.

"Take it easy, Iso. If you only had more than a primitive mortal brain stem," he teased, "you could hold up your end of both conversations."

She shot Angelo a look. He shot one right back at her. He'd been teasing, yet not teasing. He meant her to know it. He'd been oddly quiet on the entire forty-minute drive. She had no idea what had put him in such an un-angelic mood, which, she supposed, just confirmed her pea brain and aggravated him more.

Candless turned the puppy back over to a servant, one of the housemaids he'd introduced as Helena, and was carrying on about having this picture in his mind of how things should be.

Already on edge, she turned to Candless, wanting

to tell him to back off his expectations as much as she wanted to tell Angelo where he could take his attitude. "Seth will love Brandy when he gets a little bigger, I'm sure. For now, could I settle in with him for a while?"

"Of course. Halpern will bring your bags, and I will show you to your quarters. I would like him well rested to meet the rest of my family tonight."

She had to bite her tongue about what she thought about putting Seth on display. He led the way into the house, then held her elbow in a gentlemanly fashion while escorting her to the baby's suite of rooms.

Angelo had disappeared, and she was glad. Maybe he'd read her mind and taken his temper elsewhere in the universe. Moving through the house was like making her way through a museum. She could not imagine a child growing up here. When she saw the suite decked out for Seth, she felt even more appalled. There were private day-care centers, supported by outrageous tuition fees, endowed far less conspicuously than Seth's playroom, with its life-sized stuffed giraffe and a jewel-encrusted bridle on the rocking horse.

Seth was scrubbing his little eyes and fussing to be nursed. Isobel turned to Candless, who seemed to be expecting her to display wild appreciation for all he had done in preparation. "This is all a little overwhelming, Mr. Candless, I have to confess. I've honestly never seen anything like it, but the baby and I need to be alone now."

And again, he took her at her word, gracious in retreating the moment Halpern passed in the hallway to deliver her suitcases. Weary herself, she traced the chauffeur's steps to what was to be her room. She found it furnished with a skirted, king-sized bed covered in a thick peach paisley comforter, a sofa, easy chairs, each with its own oversized ottoman, a stone fireplace, and the most ornate antique cherrywood armoire and writing desk she had ever seen.

Gina Sellers would have felt very, very pampered here. Preferring her rooms in the old Victorian mansion above San Juan Capistrano, Isobel found this overmuch and stifling.

She pulled back the comforter and lay on the bed with Seth, nursing him until he fell asleep. The peacefulness she had found every other time she took the babe to her breast eluded her. She rose carefully and left him on one of the ordinary receiving blankets she had brought rather than taking him to the over-elaborate crib that still smelled of newness.

Wandering, unsettled, she avoided the windows and turned the corner into the sitting room.

Angelo sat there on the sofa, one arm stretched along the top of the cushions. His booted feet rested negligently on the thick glass coffee table. His shadowed, intense eyes fixed on her. He'd been lying in wait. He hadn't taken his attitude anywhere; instead he'd been sitting here stewing in it.

"What's wrong with you?"

"*Ovarios,* Iso," he spat, mocking Candless's admiring tone.

"You heard that?"

"I heard." He scowled deeply.

"Well, what of it, Angelo? I thought it was… clever. Flattering. Candless was only complimenting me on—"

"Your anatomy!"

"—standing up to him... Dear Lord." She began to laugh. "You're...jealous, aren't you!"

"No, Isobel," he contradicted evenly, though there was nothing especially even in his temper or his possessive look. "What I am is angry."

Chapter Seven

Isobel flushed. "Forgive my poor primitive mortal brain stem, *mi amor,* but what are you angry about? Or at whom? Candless? Are you mad? Have you lost your vaunted mind? You are behaving like a Neanderthal!"

As a matter of course, he had rendered useless every listening device given Isobel by the government agents the moment she saw him, but he was thick into his feelings and outrage. "Iso, I will not apologize. I am humorless where it comes to your honor, I concede, but I do not think 'Neanderthal' is quite accurate."

"Fine," she retorted. "Like Don Quixote, then, hopelessly stuck in an age of chivalry long, *long* since passed!"

"Oh, yeah. The man of La Mancha, dreaming the impossible dream. Now there you've caught the essence of my hopelessly medieval attitudes, but again, I do not apologize, Isobel. In our time, I would have cut out the tongue of a man who dared speak to you of something so intimate."

"You would not!"

"I would, Iso. I am the one who guarded your honor, who stopped short of—"

"Making love to me?" she cried softly, seeing now the depth and roots of his anger. "Then get over it and make love to me, here and now, and we'll both just have to suffer our tarnished reputations in heaven!"

His eyes flared and then narrowed. He swallowed, scarcely able to croak her name. "Iso. You don't—"

"I do," she insisted, meeting his look. Shivers skittered over her flesh. Her heart knocked crazily. She sank to her knees in front of him and took his hands. "I do mean it."

He swallowed. "Here."

"Now."

A vein in his mortal temple throbbed. He breathed as if the air had been sucked from his lungs. He couldn't take his eyes off her. "Iso, my God—"

He was interrupted by a sharp rap at the door. "Ms. Avedon?"

Angelo pulled away from her and got up, skirting her. Her hands balled up. She wanted to scream. "Who is it?"

"Helena, ma'am. I've been sent to see if I may bring your dinner on a tray. Is there...is someone there troubling you?"

Isobel sprang to her feet, wildly frustrated. "No," she called through the still-closed door. "Thank you, but I am not hungry."

"All right. But may I just come in and make sure everything is satisfactory?"

"Let her in, Iso," Angelo commanded harshly, his voice deep with his own thwarted desire. "She heard you talking to me. God knows what story she'll run off with if she doesn't get an explanation.''

Isobel pulled her hair back with both hands, then crossed the sitting room and jerked open the door.

Helena peeked in, then invited herself further. Isobel stepped back.

''I thought I heard voices. Yours, anyway.'' Peering up under her brow, not to be so bold as to invite a rebuke, she gave Isobel a concerned look. She had an Eastern European look about her cheeks and eyes, and a clear, pale complexion. ''You look a little bit warm. Are you certain you're all right, miss?''

Fighting for her wits, she knew she must look disastrously flushed to the maid. She was sick with disappointment at having been interrupted at such a moment.

''Embarrassed, is all,'' she improvised. ''I was comforting the baby. No. That's not true. I sometimes talk to myself aloud. My...my mother did that.''

Helena arched her head back and nodded. ''I know exactly what you mean. I sometimes sing to myself,'' she admitted.

''Well, that's much more lovely that yattering on,'' Isobel said. ''But as you can see, no one has disturbed me. Have...has the family already dined?''

''Yes. They will all be gathering soon to greet the new baby.''

Angelo stood looking out through the panes of the French doors, his stance impossibly contained. Feeling fevered and desperate to go to him, Isobel struggled to maintain her equanimity. She must deal with this, must get past the first meeting with the Candless family, and then it might be easier.

"How long?" she asked.

Helena checked the serviceable watch on her heavy-boned wrist. "Forty minutes."

"Does the household run so precisely?" Isobel asked.

"Oh, it does." Helena answered, nodding quite firmly. "Yes. It…may not be easy with the baby, but it will work out. Whatever Mr. Candless wishes works out." She looked hopefully to Isobel. "Could I see him? I only caught a glance as you came in."

Isobel could think of no reason to refuse. In her hesitation, Angelo spoke, inaudible to Helena, still facing the door. "Iso, we have to talk. Ask her to sit with the babe until he wakes. She will be deeply flattered."

Isobel took a deep, ragged breath, hoping Helena would chalk it up to an appropriate case of nerves. "Would you mind sitting with Seth until Mr. Candless comes? That way I could compose myself—"

"Oh, that would be so fine! May I?"

Isobel nodded gratefully. "Please. He is asleep in my room."

Helena hurried away through the combined play and sitting room to the bedroom. Isobel followed to thank the woman and close the door on her way out.

Alone with Angelo again, everything that had ever been at stake between them now, she went to stand before him. She understood that he had caught Helena, even the entire household, up in some warp of time to prevent an interruption again.

He looked at her, started to speak, and then gave it up, taking her into his arms instead. Fully human, he was aroused, and did not try to hide it from her or to hold her in such a way that she would not know.

Still, leaning into him, her head against his warm chest, she sensed his intention. Her throat ached, clotted with tears.

"Iso, don't cry."

"Can Helena hear us?"

"No. She will hear nothing."

Her heart twisted. "Angelo, don't do this, I beg you." She pulled back only far enough to search his eyes. "What is chastity but a useless vanity between us? Will the world stop turning or the sun burn out or heaven crumble to dust if you and I—"

"No." He cupped her cheek in his palm, stroked her tears away with his thumb. "But if I made love to you Iso, which I swear to you is the only desire in my immortal soul, I could not leave you as I must when this is done."

"Still you hold us to impossible standards!" she cried, pulling away from him.

"Try to remember that you came back for Seth, Iso, and not this."

"Don't presume to remind me, Angelo de Medici, of what I have done or why! We, you and I, would not have come to this if you had chosen to give this assignment to some other avenger."

"Then try to remember instead that it is because I love you more, not less—"

"Don't say it!" she cried, flying at him with all the pent-up fury inside her. "Don't. If you ever loved me half so much as your precious honor, we would not have been reduced to necking in the courtyard of the palace where your enemies waited to strike you down!"

He saw then that Isobel had long since recognized his unending arrogance, how he had been taken off guard because his vaunted instincts were blunted with wanting her and yet still he refused, in the name of honor, to consummate their love.

She struck her futile angry blows against his chest until he pulled her into his arms again, trapping her hands between them.

Her anger excited him past all reason. He knew what to do with her desire but not her burning anger. He wanted to make up to her what she couldn't have, or he wanted to give her something to remember…or he wanted her too much to fight her fury.

He would never know why, but he matched her passion, degree for degree. Thrusting his hand into her exquisite hair, he clenched his fist and pulled back until her lips came too near his to stop the kiss.

His mouth covered hers, his pressure forced her head back even more. It began in anger and exploded in desire for them both. His mouth watered at the taste of her, at the heat and the softness, at her answering urgency.

His tongue touched hers, their chins met. He had no recall of how it felt, his whiskers scraping her tender flesh, but emotions, memories flared and clashed in a moment out of time. He cupped her neck and deepened the kiss, and cupped her bottom and brought their bodies together more powerfully than if they had lain naked and joined together.

Isobel's anger flowed into desire and then into a tenderness too singular to be a dream. She invited and he engulfed her. He took and she gave—lavishly—and all only in the space of that kiss and the coming together of their fully clothed bodies.

He conceded his mind to her, along with his heart and his soul. He admitted in that ever-deepening kiss,

in its undertow, his arrogance and conceit. He treas-
ured her rash compassion. He cherished her spirit.
He counted her stronger than himself, strong enough
to defy heaven and earth for the sake of a mortal
infant.

All this he conveyed in their heated, wet kisses.
His unbending values were suited to a medieval pal-
adin, but with this kiss he went beyond himself, and
she finally knew what it was to be loved beyond the
physical, beyond the need to join more closely.

He was hers, body and soul, yet not hers. He belonged in his role as an Avenging Angel. She belonged with Seth. She had provoked him to this. She
would grieve its loss her whole life through.

Their kiss ended. He let her go and stood back,
dazed, backhanding the moisture from his lips and
chin, his eyes fixed darkly on hers. She backed away
and fought to breathe again. She obviously didn't
know what to say, how to act. He didn't know how
to follow his own act.

Angelo was in love with a mortal woman, and he
knew, if she didn't, that the love affair between them
was more powerful and sacred than any marriage,
and could never end. But the realization left him
powerless.

He was the mighty, resourceful Avenging Angel,
to whom no evil had ever presented too great a chal-
lenge, but in the wake of that kiss and that realization, he had no better idea how his universe worked
now than Einstein would have had, if gravity had
suddenly failed.

AT SEVEN FORTY-FIVE Ian Candless came for Isobel
and his baby son. Isobel had given Seth a bath, in

the time left her, which always put him in a warm, cuddly mood. He even smiled for Candless, and when Isobel put him into his father's arms, he was still grinning. Isobel took up her sewing basket, which concealed the listening devices that she intended to begin leaving around like a trail of bread crumbs. The basket had been an accidental stroke of genius. She didn't have much to do with her hands when she wasn't carrying Seth.

He led the way to the open-beamed living room. An exquisite Biesendorfer grand piano sat at the near end, nearly dwarfed by the size of the room. At the far end, enormous French doors on either side of a carved marble hearth looked out onto the rolling green estate, the cliffs and the churning Pacific Ocean beyond. The setting sun lent mauve and pink hues to the sky, which then reflected against the white stucco living-room walls.

The hardwood floor shone like brass polished to a high sheen. Scattered artfully about, Aubusson carpets of the highest quality broke up the expanse of floor. The finest grade of leather furniture mixed cleverly with more tailored upholstery. And art— suitable to the collections of major museums— graced the white stucco walls and antique tables.

Candless's wealth had not been underestimated. Nor, Isobel decided, could she afford to underestimate the will of the man who had created such wealth and used it to surround himself with such beauty.

She didn't need to remind herself that his behavior and mores offended her deeply, and that he was about to cause a great deal of pain to his family.

Or that he if he chose, he could dismiss her with

a wave of his hand, and keep her from Seth, and Seth from her. She would have no chance of fighting him alone.

She dared a glance at Angelo, took his look of encouragement in, breathed deeply and allowed Candless to escort her into the midst of his family.

Seven of them waited. All three sons, one with a wife, Candless's daughter and her husband, and an older woman. Candless's wife.

Not one of them pretended to be happy, but at least Bruce, the oldest son, a tall, lean, handsome dead ringer for a much younger Ian Candless, didn't take it out on Isobel with ill-concealed looks.

Standing at his mother's side—a statement of alliances, Isobel thought—Bruce shook her hand and winked in an automatic way, as if they had a secret between them. He kissed the back of her hand.

"Not many people," he said, "would have rushed in and saved young Seth, here. Not in the hail of bullets the police describe. Whatever possessed you?"

"I think you're wrong," Isobel disagreed pleasantly. This was the man who, according to Kathryn Weston, did all his father's dirty work. Interesting that he stood so close by his mother, if that was true. "I think anyone would have done what I did, if they had been there."

"A philosophical difference," he allowed, watching her closely, trying, she thought, to quickly assess what made her tick. With respect to his response, she knew better. Too many people held back in an assault, too few intervened, for fear of being hurt themselves. It had simply not occurred to her that she could be harmed, until she had been. "Maybe later you'll tell us how you happened to be there," he said.

"Hardly matters how she came to be there, does it?" Candless said, shifting Seth carefully from one arm to the other, dismissing any significance in Bruce's question. "She was. She saved my son." He turned to his wife to present his illegitimate baby. "My dear. May I present Seth?"

Patrice Candless somehow managed to be civil under very difficult circumstances. Her husband, after all, was parading about the son of one of his dalliances. Isobel flashed on Biblical stories of patriarchs presenting their wives with the child of another woman, a servant.

Hoping Patrice would emerge from this humiliation in some meaningful way, Isobel's heart went out to her. Of them all, she was the one most victimized by her husband.

"Careful," Angelo warned Isobel from his invisible vantage point. "She may be victimized, Iso, but she is strong-willed."

She would have to be, Isobel thought in answer.

Patrice tried, in fact, to take Seth from Candless's arms, asking to hold him.

He blithely refused. "In a bit, my dear. Let me first introduce my son all around." She dropped her arms, the folds of her designer blouse caving. She gave a brittle smile and Candless moved on.

"Harrison. Glad to see you could make my little soiree to greet Seth." He confided to Isobel, "Harrison had a hot date, which I'm sure it pained him a great deal to break. Or was it some never-to-be-repeated photo opportunity? Harrison, you see," he said to Isobel, "is a bit of a shutterbug."

"You wouldn't believe the photo ops out there, Dad," Harrison said. The jut of his chin was smug, but the plaintive tone of his voice robbed him of whatever punch he thought he had. "Besides. How could I miss this?" He stared with loathing at Seth.

"You couldn't, of course. Harrison is also a gambler of some repute." Seeming to speak to Isobel, he stared his son in the face. "The higher the stakes, the better, isn't that right, son? Except that you're too paranoid to really shoot for the moon."

Harrison's too-pretty face cracked in a smile. "I remember when you taught me that only the paranoid survive, Dad. Do you remember? Easter Sunday morning, 1977?"

Isobel swallowed. Harrison's humorless jibe, pitched with his plastic smile, suggested a deep pit of resentment, which Candless's reaction only confirmed. "You're whining again, Harry."

The tension rose with each in-your-face confrontation. Isobel wondered how long it would be before Seth began to absorb it and act out. Thus far he had entertained himself with Candless's tie. Maybe if he spit up or something this disastrous meeting would end.

She didn't need to see any more. She had no idea what Harrison's Easter Sunday of 1977 had been like, but Seth's life in this fabulously wealthy compound would be crowded to the open-beamed ceilings with things, and bereft of even the most basic emotional requirements.

Leaving this gathering, however, was out of the question.

Candless moved on to his middle son. "Conrad. Michele. Meet your new brother." Rising from matched hunter-green leather club chairs near the marble hearth, Conrad and his wife, Michele, stood stiffly awaiting their turn. Michele went through the motions of cooing at the baby, but her eyes and voice were flat and uncaring. Conrad ignored Isobel as well as the baby, heading to refill his glass with tequila.

"Conrad oversees IJ Candless factory personnel," Candless explained. "He's lowered our operating costs five percent this year."

Conrad ignored the faint praise. Licking, then salting his wrist and licking again, he tossed back the shot of tequila in one gulp. "It's enough to make a grown man cry, you know? Your bringing home a new baby brother and all."

Candless merely blinked. Seth patted his cheek, seeking his eyes, his attention, to no avail at all. "Your overwhelming joy is duly noted, Conrad."

"Why not, *Dad?* If this is the way you want things, my inheritance is already shot to sh—"

"Watch your mouth, will you, Connie?" Candless spat, reducing his son to the level of a three-year-old by use of the nickname.

"If I wanted to disinherit you, and God knows you've given me ample reason quite on your own," he let his eyes flicker toward Michele, "you would have been bouncing drunks to scratch out a living a long time ago."

"Oh, Daddy, stop it," Candless's pregnant daughter Kelsey interrupted, stamping her foot. "This is just hideous of you!"

Isobel took her to be the youngest, the one who would insist on attention, and get it because she was Daddy's little girl. Bruce protected his mother and did his father's dirty work, Harrison gambled and whined, wanting desperately to one-up his father, Conrad drank until he could say what was on his mind, and Kelsey sopped up the attention.

"Just let's meet the baby and get this over with. You aren't disinheriting anyone, isn't that right?"

Candless eyed his daughter. He had grimaced at her little foot-stamping gesture, and Isobel thought if she had once had can-do-no-wrong status with her Daddy, she'd lost it somewhere along the line.

"That's right, Kelsey, even if it's just some chunk of coal I leave you." He laughed out loud as if this were some long-standing joke. "This is Isobel. Isobel, Kelsey and her husband, IJ Candless counsel, Emory St. John."

"Kelsey," Isobel greeted Candless's daughter. Less good-looking than any of her brothers, she would still draw the eyes of men. She wore a delicate A-line dress and a woven leather bracelet as easily as her diamonds, which flared in the light against her country-club tan. Her waist had only begun to thicken. "Your father told me you are expecting his first grandchild. You must be very happy."

"Of course. It's all I've dreamed of, giving Daddy a grandchild." Only now her father had a new son, and Kelsey, obviously, wasn't happy at all.

Isobel turned to her husband. "Was it you, Mr. St. John, who advised Mr. Candless against acknowledging Seth as his son?"

St. John cleared his throat. Twenty or more years older than his wife, he had lizard-like eyes that constantly checked his wife's mood, and then defied it. "Yes. That was my advice. I felt strongly that it would have been the least…disruptive path."

Candless laughed. The sound wasn't jovial. "Ah,

but what a bore you are, Sinjin. What about the drama of life, eh?''

St. John sipped from a martini. Closer to Candless's age than his wife's, he behaved as if they were equals. "I prefer drama in the confines of fiction, Ian."

"And I prefer," Candless replied in a flinty tone, "to do the honorable thing."

"Then we return to our basic conflict as usual. Honor and decency aren't always in the same ballpark." St. John shrugged, and though Kelsey made him the object of a furious jab to the ribs, he ignored her. "It is honorable, for instance, to take responsibility for your actions, Ian, no matter how distasteful. It is quite another thing, indecent to my way of thinking, to foist that responsibility on your wife and family."

St. John's daring took Isobel's breath away. Angelo whistled softly. Isobel glanced toward him. He poured himself a goblet of Chardonnay, made it invisible to the gathering as well, and took a healthy swallow. "Wonder why we don't hear Candless complimenting ol' Sinjin on his *cojones*."

She nearly burst out laughing, but Angelo pointed warningly at her with the forefinger of the hand holding his wine glass. Her tension eased, even though Candless glared at his son-in-law. His complexion darkened and his eyes narrowed dangerously.

Seemingly desperate to distract her father, Kelsey interrupted. "Daddy, this is not the time. Come on. Please. We've all done as you asked and gathered to meet Seth and Isobel. We don't need to add to the—"

"To the what, Kelsey?" Candless demanded softly.

"The…tension, Daddy. It's too much. We don't need you and Sinjin getting into some ridiculous moral debate."

"Well, there you have it from the horse's mouth. Kelsey is uninterested in morals," Conrad muttered darkly, his voice filled with some kind of fear of his sister.

"That's not true!" Anger flashed in Kelsey's eyes. Isobel thought she cared too much for the opinion of her brothers and father. It obviously hurt her to be criticized by him.

Bruce stood up for her. "She's right, Dad," he said, pouring his mother a glass of wine, then one for himself. "I think it's time we let Isobel tell us about herself if she's to be our little brother's nanny."

Although Candless had been ready to deliver some scathing remark to St. John, he shrugged and couched his warning in a lighter tone. "Try and remember who signs your paycheck, Sinjin."

He started to hand the baby to Isobel. Patrice put down her wine and began to cross the plush dove-gray carpeting. "Let me hold him now."

Candless relented and handed Seth over to her. He called for a staff assistant, Isobel had no idea from where, to come and take several photos of the assembled family. One or more would be issued with a press release, acknowledging that the newest Candless heir and his nanny had been found and had safely joined the family.

Isobel knew there was no escaping this, but she hated every second of it. The ill feelings among Candless's family were hardly concealed. Seth, however, was doing remarkably well. She wondered if Angelo had anything to do with the baby's good behavior, but he denied it. He poured his invisible self another invisible glass of wine, then sat at the piano. He began to play a thin, haunting tune with only one hand, echoes of a musical canon she recalled but could not place.

No key depressed. No sound played for anyone's ears but hers. It was as if he merely thought the plaintive melody, and she heard it through the strings of the instrument. His eyes fixed on her, hers on him. "I haven't done a thing to influence the baby's behavior, Iso."

She nodded distractedly, struggling to make it seem as if her nod had something to do with Bruce's suggestion.

Patrice invited them all to sit down; everyone but Harrison complied. Bruce took the baby from his mother, long enough for her to settle into her antique Queen Anne chair. She looked to Isobel. "Tell us about yourself, my dear."

"Yes, Isobel," Kelsey purred. "Helena tells us you've no baby bottles."

Isobel swallowed. "No, I—"

Lighting a cigar clipped exactly so, a scowling Candless interrupted her. "What the hell are you talking about, Kelsey? Do you think the rest of us want to sit around here listening to you prattle on about baby formulas?"

"Why, that's exactly the point, Daddy. Seth isn't on any formula at all." She turned to Isobel. "Helena says Seth smells as if he is breast-fed. Is that true?"

Chapter Eight

Isobel froze.

Candless looked taken aback, his daughter vaguely triumphant, his wife and sons embarrassed but dying to hear what Isobel would say next. What were the chances, after all, that a woman who only happened to be close enough to rescue a baby in mortal danger would also be able to breast-feed him?

Her heart skipped beat after beat. She had never been more blindsided or less prepared for a question that so efficiently sliced through the heart of her necessary lies.

"Say yes, Iso," Angelo commanded, to draw her beyond her shock. "Say it's true."

"Yes," she repeated numbly. "It's true."

"Well, how very extraordinary!" Kelsey chimed. "Not only were you Johnny-on-the-spot at the murder scene, but you came with functioning breasts."

No explanation came to Isobel's mind. It was a gift, she supposed, some physical reckoning with the metaphysical, that when she plunged into her human existence, her body came prepared to nurse the baby.

She had no idea what to say, and yet her credibility depended upon it.

"Stick it to them, Iso. Embarrass them." Angelo continued, giving her a reasonable explanation to recite. "Tell them your last position was as wet nurse to a baby whose mother died in childbirth. And say it," he urged her, "as if you consider her question beneath contempt."

"I'm sorry," Isobel began, anger catching up with her now. How had Angelo become so adept, so sure, such a skilled liar, when lies were forbidden an angel? "I didn't realize the topic of my breast-feeding Seth would become an issue."

She'd managed to provoke an uncomfortable silence. She let the moment draw itself out painfully. Not one of them met her eyes, or anyone else's either.

"Indulge us with an explanation," St. John insisted, gathering his wife's approval and Candless's reluctant nod.

"It's not so extraordinary at all." Her chin went up. "There are shots—hormones—a woman can take to begin producing milk. My last position was as a wet nurse for a baby whose mother died in childbirth. Would you like to know more?"

St. John lowered his eyes, Candless coughed and Kelsey backed off, shaking her head, swallowing her venomous look. She was pregnant. She didn't want to hear about childbirth disasters, and while Isobel's explanation wasn't a true story, there were hundreds like it that were.

Kelsey Candless St. John had never, Isobel was sure, had to face anything much more upsetting than a broken fingernail, until now. Until her father brought home a new baby that threatened them all.

"She's running scared," Angelo agreed softly. He

had stopped playing the piano. "She's a smart cookie and she sees the handwriting on the wall. Producing a grandchild might have restored her to her father's favor—or, at the very least, kept her comfortable if Candless decides to skip a generation and leave his fortune to his grandchild. Seth blows that hope to kingdom come." He stood now, unseen and unheard, and moved to the green marble hearth so that when Iso looked at him, the direction of her gaze would not cause suspicion. "Get out your sewing," he added, "and press your advantage."

She didn't want to press the narrow advantage.

He said he knew that.

She didn't want to do anything but get up and take the baby back to her rooms, away from this family who would rather have taken a snarling rabid animal into their midst than their father's illegitimate son and his nanny.

Angelo agreed she had every right to want to get away.

She would have come up with another thought, but he preempted her.

"You have to stand up to them, Iso, or they will eat you alive."

She knew he was right. She must make a stand, draw a line in the sand. Staying with Seth depended on keeping Candless's respect.

"Really, please ask," she went on, following up on Angelo's warning and her own question to them all. She drew out a square of material on which she'd started to embroider. She brought her threaded needle up through the fabric, then let her gaze rest in turn on each member of Ian Candless's family. "If you have any other questions, maybe we should get them out into the open now.''

Kelsey's expression hardened. "I assume you can prove this, provide the names and dates—"

Candless exploded in impatience. "Stop this right now," he ordered his daughter. "Your claws are showing, my pet, and it is a most unattractive sight. If you have a point to make, spit it out."

"I just think it's terribly convenient, Daddy. Think about it. If something smells in Denmark, it's because something *smells*."

"Oh, this is rich," Harrison sniped at his sister. "Kelsey mangling Shakespeare—who lived in an age, I might add, when wet nurses were the rule. Give it a rest, Kels."

Candless sat in his high-backed chair reveling, Isobel thought, in the strife he had caused. Bruce shot Harrison a look to shut him up, then cajoled his sister. "I think you owe Isobel an apology, Kelsey. She's obviously entirely legitimate."

"Unlike the kid, you mean," Conrad tossed out.

"Yes, Connie, unlike Seth," Candless agreed, "who, unlike the rest of you, may turn out to be worth a tinker's damn."

"Daddy, you don't mean that! And I didn't mean to suggest that Isobel—"

"The hell you didn't," her father interrupted contentiously. "Why don't you simply come out with it? Seth hardly resembles any of you."

"Well, he doesn't!"

"You may regard that as proof of some idiotic notion that he is not my son, but I assure you, the lab which performed the paternity testing is the finest anywhere in the world."

Isobel stared at him. His doting glance lit often on Seth, but he had deliberately added fuel to the fire, wrecking Bruce's attempt to get his siblings under control.

"Apologize to Ms. Avedon, Kels," Bruce urged again, "and be done with it."

Several looks passed back and forth before Bruce finally won out. Kelsey turned to Isobel. "I apologize. Maybe what I asked was uncalled-for. But, I mean, who could have guessed? I've never even heard of a wet nurse outside of movies."

Bruce laughed out loud, looking sheepish, purposely, Isobel thought, defusing the tension. "I'll go you one better, Kels. I never even knew what a wet nurse was."

"Stop. You're joking," his mother scolded.

"And why would I know, Mother? I admit I've an irrational fondness for the anatomy, but as to function... I'd no idea women went around doing that for other women's babies."

Patrice rolled her eyes as if this were her most incorrigible offspring, but Isobel saw that she was obviously fond of him. Charm spilled naturally out of him. "Gormley" is what Isobel's fellow Brit guardians would have called it. That sort of self-deprecating, devastatingly sexual, aw-shucks, irrepressible, lock-of-hair-on-the-forehead routine of a Hugh Grant type worked splendidly with most women. Bruce had it in spades.

She could see why Patrice Candless would dote on her eldest son, but Isobel mistrusted him. He was in some kind of pitched battle with his father over the loyalty of his brothers and sister. Patrice was already clearly in his camp, but if he had handled his father's peccadilloes, even to protect his mother, was he capable of handling them to death?

Candless's daughter had wicked instincts, a ruthlessness about her as well. She would as soon drown Seth, Isobel thought, as look at him. Would she have it in her to hire Gina Sellers's murderer?

Or Conrad? Perhaps the timid, paranoid Harrison? Isobel's mind reeled. It could be any one of them, or none. But any man who could even conceive of putting his family through such a wringer as this could expect little more.

She wouldn't stand by and watch Seth grow into another version of Bruce or Conrad or Harrison. If anyone thought Isobel would stay long at this ball, they had another think coming.

THE FOLLOWING MORNING, Halpern drove Isobel—and Angelo, though the chauffeur didn't know it—to the police station. She gave her statement and answered questions for hours. She knew she could be of little help. The only thing she had been interested in was saving Seth from sharing his mother's fate. Isobel couldn't tell them which house Gina had come from, or much of anything, other than the fact that the gunmen were Hispanic.

She gave them the identical reasons in the same words that she had used to explain her presence in the barrio neighborhood to the Candless family the night before. They took her through her story twice, confirming that it was in fact a drug deal that she had stumbled into in the shoe-repair shop.

Beyond that, she knew nothing, and by noon the police let her leave with Halpern.

After the family meeting to introduce Seth, which

provoked the kind of backbiting reaction Caroline Mapes had predicted, the family members settled into a kind of armed truce. Whether Isobel's presence motivated some sort of code of silence or what, the agents couldn't tell. It appeared to them that the family had drawn its wagons into a circle.

Still, there were little things evident in passages Angelo appropriated from the tapes. He could listen to them at twice the speed of sound, accessing the tapes by remote cell phone, so it wasn't much of a trick to pull together the telling snippets.

Harrison got drunk that same night and lost a small fortune—along with his hot date—in a private gambling club. The chauffeur went on about it at length to the mechanic who spent his days fine-tuning the thirty-seven cars belonging to various family members.

Conrad spent two nights at the office, and Michele left town in a huff. Kelsey fired her maid. St. John hired the tearful woman back, and wasn't pleased at having to mop up Kelsey's mess with the domestic help.

The agents had no way to relay this information to Isobel, which they had considered to be a problem, but it wasn't. Angelo followed their progress almost hourly, and in spare moments, reproduced conversations at will for her from thin air.

Among the siblings, Bruce was the only one who went out of his way to be friendly during meals, asking if there was anything Isobel wanted or needed, expressing an interest in and holding Seth.

But alone with Angelo their fifth night on the Candless estate, distracted and discouraged, Isobel went about picking up toys from the floor while Angelo sat in the rocker, quietly turning pages of a book with Seth.

"What are you thinking, Iso?" he asked.

She unloaded an armful of designer, stuffed alphabet blocks into one of the toy boxes and plunked down on the thick, peach-colored carpet. "This is going nowhere, Angelo." She was referring to both her relationship with him and the investigation into Gina's murder.

He arched an eyebrow at her. "It's only been five days."

"I know how long it's been." She saw that he would only talk about the Candless issues. It was a start.

"What is the point of my being here? It's as if after that first night, they all went secretly off somewhere and agreed that the best strategy is to simply ignore what Candless has done by bringing Seth here. So what if everyone is on edge? Why wouldn't they be? How is this helping to resolve Gina's murder?"

"It's not. At least not directly."

"What would you be doing differently if I were not involved, if you didn't have to hang around making sure no harm came to us?"

Since their kiss, while Helena stayed with Seth, there had been no others. He had not touched her. He'd been careful to keep his smoldering looks from her.

Every time she looked at him, she wanted more of his kisses. Every time she came upon him smiling at the baby, she wished Seth were his. Every time she opened her mouth to speak, it was to plead their case.

She never did.

He gave a half smile, adjusting Seth's small body more comfortably in his lap. "There is no telling, Iso, since you are here. But I think you underestimate the potential here."

"How?"

He looked closely at her. "Can't you feel it, really?"

"With my primitive mortal brain stem, you mean?"

"Even you, poor mortal, yes," he teased, then grew serious. "It's like they're sitting on a powder keg, Iso, but they can't see where the flare is coming from that is going to set it off."

"Do you mean all of Candless's adult children?"

Angelo nodded. "And the spouses."

"But there are tensions like this in every family, Angelo. What does it prove? That they're ordinary, that's all. Subject to the same stresses as anyone else."

"There are other things." Seth twisted in his lap, and Angelo picked him up and laid him against his shoulder. "St. John is tearing his hair out, trying to figure your angle, but he's got his hands full. The Feds picked up a handful of illegal immigrants crossing back over the border."

She didn't question how he knew this. He must have somehow been there, in his spectral form, to see it happen. "Why is that trouble?"

"Because one of the illegals was beaten up pretty badly and is not in a mood to keep his mouth shut."

"What can he tell them?"

"That his way into this country was paid. That he was working in a clothing factory in south central Los Angeles. The Feds already suspect a clothing plant belonging to Candless Industries. It's his word against a Candless spokesman, of course, as to whether they paid to get him here, or knew he was illegal, but word gets around and then there are more malcontents to deal with.''

The connection of illegal immigrants to Seth's mother was just so nebulous. Except that the Feds had recruited Gina, Isobel wouldn't have believed there could be any ties at all. But Angelo obviously believed the illegals trying to escape back across the border meant something. "What does that have to do with Gina's murder?''

"The gunmen were illegals, Iso.''

Even before he'd answered, she knew. "Couldn't they be hired anywhere, though? I mean, they wouldn't have to come from the pool IJ Candless smuggles in.''

"True. In fact, it would be better if they didn't have any Candless contact. They could pretty easily be traced back. But here's the thing. Do you know the theory behind *Six Degrees of Separation*?''

"Yes, but—''

"Think of it, Iso. It's mathematically sound. It means human beings are only six people away from knowing every other human being on earth. 'A' knows six people and 'B' is one of them. 'B' knows six more people and 'C' is one of them, all the way to 'F,' at which point you've accounted for every living human being.''

Seth had raised his head from Angelo's shoulder and was watching him with such rapt attention that Isobel laughed. Angelo lifted the baby to his face and they nuzzled. "Seth knows where I'm going with this, don't you, big guy?''

"So do I," Isobel protested. But her mouth had gone dry, wanting that easy intimacy for herself, too.

He tucked Seth back onto his shoulder. Seth stuck his thumb in his mouth and rested his head. Angelo's dark, shadowed eyes met hers. "Do you, Iso?"

For a moment she couldn't remember. It was within his powers to hear her thoughts, as easily as the seagulls cawing half a mile away, or the tinkling of wind chimes in Tibet. She didn't think he could read her thoughts often, except when she couldn't speak in front of others. She believed he had heard her now, her longing for the nuzzling he so naturally gave to Seth.

What good would it do to admit her longing, or that she had even had the thought? He had turned her away, and he would keep turning her away. She couldn't bear it.

She broke off her eye contact with him. Her head dipped low and she forced herself to return to his point. "What you're saying, I think, is that once you get into smuggling illegals, or exploiting them, the world sort of shrinks. Now you don't have to know someone who knows someone six times removed. Now the person you hire to commit a murder is likely to know someone who knows who brought them illegally across the border in the first place."

"Exactly." His eyes had grown carefully neutral. "So even if whoever hired the gunmen took every possible precaution to find men unknown to any Candless enterprise, chances are good one man knew the next, and if the police are clever, they will connect the dots and Gina's murder will lead straight back to IJ Candless."

"Have the gunmen admitted anything?"

"No." He shifted the forearm supporting Seth and began rubbing gentle circles over his backside. "These are tough *hombres,* Iso. They haven't so much as admitted to holding the guns, when the burn marks are right there on their hands. But the guy they caught trying to cross back over last night is squawking. Loudly."

"But the police haven't made the connection?"

"No."

"How can you let this go on, Angelo?" With everything in her, she appealed to his sense of justice. She didn't want Seth here one heartbeat longer than he had to be. "Isn't it in your powers to make them spill the truth? Can't you strike such fear into Candless's family that the guilty party falls all over himself confessing? What good are you, really?"

He glowered at her. No one had ever taken him to task about his abilities as an Avenging Angel. No one. "These are not easy matters, Isobel. Suppose I exercised that power. Suppose I became so enamored of my own righteousness that I took every decision into my own hands. What could stop me from making the Pope cop to some terrible crime for my own amusement?"

"That's a ridiculous exaggeration," she snapped. "In—"

"It is not such a stretch as you might imagine, Iso. There are mighty forces on the side of evil, a battle being waged between the light and the dark for all our souls." He paused. "You know it's true."

"But you are different. You would not go over to the side of evil."

"You chose to leave," he said, just as quickly, "and return here for the sake of this child. I could choose to abuse my powers, and it would take a small army of the most powerful angels to defeat me. We are not immune to temptation, Isobel.''

Oh, but he was, wasn't he? Isobel thought bitterly. Immune to her. Angelo de Medici was immune to any temptation that might compromise his almighty image of who he was.

His eyes narrowed dangerously. He knew the train of her thoughts, or he could guess. Again, she clamped her lips shut against speaking them aloud.

"Then what is next? What can we do? I can't stand sitting around this place waiting for something to crack open. Couldn't you at least connect the dots for the police?''

"We have to let this play out, Iso. The informant is an illegal. After everything that has gone down in this city in the last few years, they have to be able to prove their charges—especially against a family as powerful and wealthy as this one. But the pressure is on St. John and whoever started running those factories with illegals, because sooner or later the press will draw the connection.''

"Maybe the Feds have already got their break, then, and they don't need me here at all.''

"They do, Iso. They need all the help they can get. Like it or not, Seth represents a threat to this family, and the worse things get, the more likely they'll crack wide open.''

"I don't like it. I don't want to be here when that happens, I don't want—''

"I know, Iso. I understand.''

She swept her hair back and took a deep breath. He understood too well and it tired her to know that his understanding her made no difference.

"What did you mean earlier when you said St. John is tearing his hair out trying to figure my angle?"

"It's beyond his world view, Iso, to imagine anyone voluntarily throwing themselves into harm's way to save a life. But now you have gone and begged to be allowed to take care of a child that a week ago you didn't even know existed. He doesn't even buy comfort and money as a motive."

"Have I been transparent with my feelings about Ian Candless?"

"Not so much. You are naturally skeptical. St. John respects that, but he nevertheless believes you have some secret agenda for being here, Iso. And of course, he is right."

She got up from the floor and went to cup the baby's head in her hand, to feel his soft curls. She needed no reminder of her agenda. She wanted this baby, a chance to nurture and care for him herself. But now her needs had grown beyond her original goal, and she couldn't imagine a future without Angelo there to cradle Seth to his shoulder, coaxing him to sleep by the sounds and deep, soothing vibrations of his voice alone.

She should never have come this close. The babe's essence was so small and tender and warm, but the essence of the man, so large and powerful and arrogant—and hot—brought her to her knees.

"Angelo."

She wanted to sink to the floor again, to let her head rest against his thigh and her hands in the stiff folds of his jeans. Her pulse thumped till she could hear her own heartbeat. She wanted him to be mortal, to comfort her, to take her to his breast as he had

Seth, only to make love to her till Hell froze over and the triumph of good over evil was no longer at stake.

But she knew she would have him only long after Hell had already frozen over, and she pretended it didn't matter. "Stay with him a little longer? I just want to go...to the kitchen."

"Whatever you want, Iso, you can have right here."

"You mean you'll conjure it?" She barely prevented herself from bursting into hysterical laughter. He would not conjure the only thing she truly wanted. "No. I can't have what I want right here. You see, what I want is to brew a cup of tea for myself."

"Then go." His voice was deeper, harsher than she had ever known. If he knew what was in her heart and her thoughts, then it had reason to be. She wanted more than anything to be away from him, where she could envision a life without him. "Seth and I will be fine," he said.

And so will I, she thought fiercely. *So will I, when you are gone and all that is left for me is Seth.*

Chapter Nine

"She is whistling in the dark, *mon ami*," Pascal said. "Past the graveyard of her dreams."

"What are you doing here?" Angelo asked, deeply annoyed, moderating his tone so as not to disturb Seth, who lay now fully stretched out over the length of his torso.

Insouciant as hell, Pascal leaned against the frame of the French doors, watching Isobel cross the courtyard to the kitchen. "You have been too preoccupied to check in with me, so I put aside all matters pressing and not so pressing to come to you. The mountain to Mohammed, so to speak."

"Let me guess. As the French say?"

"*Oui. Que sera, sera.* The mountain to Mohammed. It is my solemn duty to appropriate to the French whatever suits us, whenever it suits us."

"I would suggest a soupçon of integrity."

"Oh-ho!" Pascal chortled. "Your soul and your...persona, shall we say, are so far out of synch as to be virtual strangers, and you have the gall to speak of integrity to me?"

Angelo sighed a very bored and angry mortal sigh. "What do you want, Pascal? What will satisfy you?"

Pascal shrugged elaborately. "That you get your head on straight. That would make me—" He kissed his fingertips and let his fingers splay joyfully. "That would make me very happy."

"I am an Avenging Angel—"

"Ah, yes. But your contentment just now, cuddling the baby, belies your belief, like some Saturday morning American cartoon character, that the fate of all mankind lies in your hands."

"Maybe it does," Angelo snapped, the babe sleeping blissfully on his chest, "if you are representative of the rest." He knew as he said it that if Pascal were truly representative of all the rest, the world's ills would have long since passed away, but he felt as if he were being attacked. Defensive and churlish because of it.

"Careful, Angelo," Pascal warned. "I did not come to take your ill-tempered abuse. And if I must, I shall intervene to spare Isobel as well."

He ignored the threat. "I have not been ill-tempered with her—"

"No. Only a sanctimonious ass. The result is the same, I fear. Soon you will be without friend or lover. Don't worry. God will still love you."

Angelo glowered. "You go too far, Pascal."

"Au contraire. I have yet to begin," he returned with deep feeling. "Have you thought perhaps that it is you who do not go far enough? Have you considered, even for a second, that there may be higher values to embrace than justice?"

Angelo had forty scathingly brilliant comebacks, none of which, however, would have sufficed to silence Pascal. He was no saint. Angels rarely were. But Pascal had invented the sentiment himself.

He sinned, he swore, he lusted, he bragged, he cheated and lied with impunity. Not once in the fifty-odd years that he had been among the Avenging Angels had he suffered the slightest consequence of flouting all the rules. In fact, he directed International, and it was Angelo who had lobbied hard to get Pascal into the position of leadership.

There were others more fearsome, Angelo among them, but Pascal was wily, dedicated and heartful. His sinning was ever in the service of mankind, and he never, ever let a halo in his jurisdiction kid himself that justice was the be-all and end-all of a world gone mad.

Love was the answer. There wasn't any other way for the human race to stop killing itself off and come together. Pascal knew it, preached it when he got the chance—playing at whatever pulpit he found temporarily empty—and now he was in Angelo's face with it.

Angelo lowered his head, angling to touch his cheek to Seth's warm curls, and for a moment he was so enamored of the baby, and of the smell of Isobel lingering on his sweet breath, that he nearly forgot Pascal was there.

His anger had melted away, but it didn't change anything. He didn't know who he was if not an Avenging Angel of the Lord, dedicated, devoted to restoring justice. Let the choirs of angels and the cherubs and guardians—even Pascal—attack the hell that was earth by teaching only love. Angelo de Medici could not.

"You do yourself a grave disservice, *mon ami*," Pascal murmured. "In five hundred years you have become more fearsome than the Archangel Michael casting Lucifer from Heaven, but still you will not admit to your consciousness the miracle of sitting there holding the babe in his sleep.''

Angelo flushed darkly. ''That is a cheap shot, Pascal.''

Pascal laughed. ''I have been called many things, Angelo, but never the lobber of cheap shots.'' He moved across the room, soaking up vibes like a sponge soaking nutrients from the sea. ''I thought you should know you were right.''

''About the informant?'' Angelo queried. His one and only report to Pascal, in the form of a dispatch through the ether, had addressed this issue.

''*Oui*. The man who was beaten and now accuses Candless Industries is a liar.''

Angelo looked sharply to Pascal. The baby startled, lifted his head and gave a cry, then just as swiftly fell back to sleep. ''Who put him up to it? The government?''

''It would not be the first time,'' Pascal agreed. ''The strategy is simple. A phony charge—well publicized—encourages anyone with an ax to grind, and who was truly brought illegally across the border, to come forward.''

Angelo nodded slowly. Easier by far for anyone, he thought, to join in such accusations than to break the silence first. Among illegal immigrants, who knew they could be summarily deported in the blink of an eye, this was especially true.

''Does this liar of an informant know anyone who was actually brought across by Candless Industries?''

''If it is, in fact, occurring that Candless is importing illegals, then almost certainly he does. But it would be very foolish indeed to squeal on them. He would find himself very dead very quickly.''

''It would be a stupid risk,'' Angelo agreed. He had spent hours away from Isobel—when she was sleeping deeply and a fraction of his attention was enough to watch over her—searching among the illegals for those men and women bought and paid for with Candless money. There were too many, and they were all too closemouthed. One careless word...

It wasn't, as Isobel worried, that he had done nothing. He had even gone, during those hours when she rested, to the jail where the men who had murdered Gina were still being incarcerated.

They spoke to no one. Their hearts and minds were branded with a fear of American authorities. They knew the tricks, the promises of immunity or even citizenship, the good-cop bad-cop routines. Where they came from, such tricks were staples elevated to an art form.

An American prison was a hundred times better than being deported, tossed back into the poverty and corruption they had fled, and they knew it.

''If all that is true,'' Pascal said, having followed Angelo's train of thought, ''then it is certain the informant is a plant.''

''Or a man who suspects he is already dead meat—''

''At the hands of his compatriots,'' Pascal finished. Among the men and women of the French Resistance, there had been no offense so heinous as betraying a brother in the cause. In much the same way, the illegal immigrants stood together, all for one, one for all. Especially those who had been brought across and given employment and housing from the start.

But Pascal cared for none of this discussion. Angelo could see he was letting the subject wander where it might, but he was not yet finished with what he had earlier begun.

Angelo rose from the easy chair where he had slouched to accommodate Seth's small body. He turned the babe over, cradling Seth's head in his hand, supporting his small, slumbering body against the length of his forearm. Taking the baby to his crib, he eased the child back onto his side, patted his diapered behind, and turned to face Pascal.

"Why don't you ask it?"

Pascal's brow hiked, his obnoxious *what, me?* expression taking over. "What question would that be, *mon ami?*"

Angelo sighed in his mortal weariness at Pascal's games. He materialized a serving of Portuguese wine for himself, knocking back half the goblet. "I have it within my power to elicit the information I want. What stops me?"

"This is true. You need only present yourself to the illegals as one of them. They would believe you, and spill their guts to you."

"Or single out one of them and, by my willpower alone, maneuver the hapless victim into a corner where all hope of escape is gone. A place where, again, spilling the truth is the only option left."

"So then, Angelo, what does stop you, other than your preference to stay here, confined in this lovely marriage of convenience with Isobel?"

SHE WANDERED across the courtyard to the kitchen patio. The path between them, lit by an occasional decorative lantern and fragrant with the scent of deep banks of flowers, wended its way across the lawn, this way and that. Not the most direct route, but more private and shorter than through the house.

Hoping to soothe herself, Isobel breathed in the scents of the flowers and the spray of sea water crashing against the cliff side. A haze of fog covered the full moon. Dark clouds lined in silver by the moonlight hung stubbornly in place.

There were times, Isobel remembered, when she had taken her angel consciousness into the thick of such clouds and back out again, to remind herself that she was a light unto the darkness, that it was within her powers to change the quality of a life, the essence of being, the dark, uneasy, even menacing thoughts of mortals by the light she brought to bear in their hearts and minds.

Sometimes, in clouds as dark as these it was easier to see her powers metaphorically at work than in a human soul. Angelo was reacting to her now with equally complicated emotions, and she could not find her own light. She had traded it in for her human existence, and she had no power to pierce his reason.

All she understood clearly was that he would rather honor the reputation of the woman she had ceased to be five hundred years ago than love her now. And Angelo de Medici always had what he'd rather.

Let him, she thought fiercely, fully, humanly, womanly—thoroughly angry for the first time in this or any age. *Let him rot in his honor, or let him flaunt it forever after.* Isobel Avedon was through being the object of his restraint.

She came to the kitchen door, punched in the security code she had been given and turned the brass doorknob. Ian and the family had gone off to some celebrity charity function for the night, but she knew Candless employees could and surely were instructed to follow her every move.

Her specific codes pinpointed her location more accurately than if she had gone through the house, but even then, the motion detectors triggered hidden cameras. Angelo had pointed out the locations of a few of them.

She didn't bother looking for others. They were so cleverly concealed that unless you knew they were there, you simply didn't see them. It was safer to assume that she was being watched at every moment.

The only way to defeat the system was to provide motion and images for the cameras. Though she could not do this, Angelo could, and did. When she was supposedly alone in Seth's nursery suite, Angelo provided moving holographic images of her napping or sewing or writing at the small antique rolltop in her own room.

She found the cameras unfathomable and creepy and worse, invasive. Her image as an angel could not be captured, but she no longer had that advantage. She understood what it was for primitives to believe that their essence was caught and stolen by such contrivances.

Her essence could not be stolen, or her thoughts invaded, so let them watch her brew her tea and take it outside to sit in the porch swing on the gazebo, looking out to the ocean.

But when she had filled a ceramic teapot in the darkened kitchen and put it on the gas burner, then turned around to get a tea bag from the small brass canister, a ticking sound too near and too ominous drove away all thoughts of taking her cup of tea to the gazebo. The ticking alarmed her deeply, and she froze. When the noise ceased, she turned slowly.

Harrison Candless sat at the glass-top kitchen table with a bottle of tequila and a revolver, alternately spinning the cylinder and pulling the trigger. He aimed at nothing, not himself, not her, just sideways while he watched the hammer slam home in the dark. But he was watching her.

Her heart hammered in her throat. She wondered how the cameras had failed to pick him up. Why estate security had not come to take the gun away from him. Perhaps the cameras in the service areas of the house only monitored the entrances. He would know where he could sit drinking and contemplating his own death without leaving the house or risking interference.

The digital clock read 11:30. "Harry?" she said. "Are you okay?"

He snorted, spinning the chamber with his thumb, reaching with his left hand to pour himself another shot of tequila. "Okay? Relative, isn' it?" He giggled softly. "Everything's relative. Everyone's relative. Can't get away from 'em."

"Your family, you mean?"

"Uuuu-biquitous. Family. Yeah, tha's what I mean all right."

"Harry, you really should put the gun down. Please. Just put it down."

"S'not loaded." He shrugged. She could have sworn that tears glittered in his eyes. "See, there's the bullet. Only brought one along—'f I miss once, I won't be in any shape to use an—nother one.''

"Harry—"

"Harrison!" he barked. "My freaking name is Harrison Blain Galsworthy Candless.''

"Harrison, then." She believed what he'd said was true, that the gun wasn't yet loaded, but he was teetering on some indefinable edge. And she could be wrong in believing him.

She had to talk him out of this. She removed a tea bag and replaced the canister on the marble tile countertop. "Can I fix you a cup of tea?"

"—'m not as drunk as I sound.''

"You don't have to be to want a cup of hot tea, or...do you want to just talk?''

"Confess, you mean, Saint Isobel?" Again he breathed out through his nose in that disdainful snort. He spun the chamber over and over, then looked straight into her eyes. "Who are you? Where did you come from?''

For a split second she thought he knew exactly who and what she was, or had been. What else had she done to be called Saint Isobel? "I'm just an ordinary woman, not a saint or even your confessor. But I am a good listener.''

He shook his head. "Too much to tell, Ms. Avedon. Wouldn't know where to start or where to stop.''

He would talk, she thought, if only she could offer him a place to begin. The teapot began to whistle. She shut off the fire and strung the tea bag into the water to steep, then turned back. "How about Easter Sunday, 1977.''

Still staring at her, he gulped, then his jaw jutted

out. He was on the edge, sick at heart and a little too drunk on tequila and some private grief to think whether he should spill his pain or not. "Let's see. Easter Sunday, 1977. Took my licks and kept on tickin'." He laughed sourly at his bit of poetic license. "Easter Sunday. See, it fell on my birthday that year. I was seven years old."

Isobel thought about what a sweet age that could be, how loving seven-year-old boys were. But she didn't think Harrison's story was leading anywhere particularly sweet.

His eyes closed tight for a minute. She thought he was fighting off tears. "What did you get for your birthday?"

"The old man bought me a baseball bat. Had all these autographs on it."

"Was a baseball bat with autographs what you wanted?"

"More than anything."

"But then something happened to ruin your birthday?"

"You could say that." He sniffed. His handsome face twisted in a grimace. His thumb toyed idly with the chamber of the gun, spinning it. "Old Ian pitched till I couldn't swing anymore, and then he pitched some more. The only time I hit the freaking ball, I hit him in the face with it." He gave that desperate little snort again. "See, he really wasn't lookin', 'cause he never expected me to connect. Didn't even get a black eye, tha's how pathetic it was."

Isobel poured her tea and sat down across the table from Harrison. Her throat tightened. There was no way she could look at Ian Candless's adult son and not see the little boy, the baby he had once been.

Or Seth.

"What happened then?"

"He flew into a rage. Picked up the ball and threw it at me, hard's he could."

She couldn't help flinching. "He hit you with a baseball?"

"Yeah. See, I thought he was pitching. I'd miss, and then I'd chase it down and throw it back to him." He choked. "Smart kid, huh? Took me about ten times to figure out he was doin' it on purpose, hittin' me with that freaking ball."

Isobel clamped her lips shut. Her body cringed with the same sense of betrayal that must have consumed Harrison, the shame and humiliation and rage at being his father's all-too-trusting target.

Ian Candless had made a believer of his youngest son at the ripe old age of seven.

Only the paranoid survive.

The sentiment ruled his life, she could see that. He took the risks, and if he was too paranoid or paralyzed to go for broke, then he had his father to thank for that too.

Ian Candless hadn't changed, either. Kathryn Weston—and all the men in the Brentwood Smoking Club, where Angelo sometimes went—might have been correct in saying that Candless was a paragon of virtue in his business dealings. But he'd crippled his youngest son with fear, rubbed his family's noses in his infidelities, and provoked ill will between his adult children for the perverse pleasure of seeing them squabbling over a fortune that might end up going to an illegitimate contender.

After all they had been through.

Harrison Candless felt threatened by Seth. God

only knew what he would do, or what he had done. Something was eating him alive with guilt or he wouldn't be sitting here planning to blow himself to hell in the kitchen of his father's estate.

Isobel sat back, took a deep breath and steeled herself. "Harrison, did you have anything to do with the murder of Seth's mother?"

He could only look at her. She couldn't read the slightest emotion in his face—not guilt, knowledge or innocence. She didn't know him well enough to guess what impassive, total control meant.

He picked up the bullet and shoved it into one of the grooves, then knocked the chamber into place. "When are you going to make your play, Saint Isobel?"

She swallowed hard. "I don't know what you mean."

"I don't know what you mean," he mimicked softly. "I think you do." His handsome face drew into an even nastier twist. A lock of his blond hair fell over his forehead. He was seeming a lot less drunk now, and far more focused. "I think you have it planned down to the gnat's ass. I think you're just waiting till we all get a really stinking good feel for what it's going to be like having precious little Seth around for the next twenty years."

Bile stung her throat. The bitter taste triggered deadly memories in her soul. Angelo de Medici was a strong and powerful man, a man to be reckoned with, a man his enemies had feared. A man, nevertheless, murdered in an unguarded moment.

An unguarded moment devoted to her.

Guilt threatened to swamp her. Like a predator, the memory caught her by the throat, struck her dumb; but her fear now was for Seth. She still had no idea what Harrison meant, what he expected her to say, but her delay in answering made him crazier.

"How *much?*" he snarled, throwing the gun down on the glass-top table, relishing the intimidating clatter of metal against glass. "What's it going to take to get you and that little bastard out of here?"

Isobel flinched, fighting to breathe. The gun unnerved her. Harrison Candless's meaning chilled her to her mortal marrow. "What was Gina asking?"

"Sellers wanted five million. What's your price?"

Isobel fought the chill, the numbness. "Harrison, was Gina Sellers murdered so you wouldn't have to come up with that kind of money? Is that the way this works? If you can afford what I want, okay, but if not, I'm dead too?"

He laughed at her. "I'm the coward, remember? I'm the one who...oh, forget it." He swigged straight from the bottle of tequila. He gritted his teeth. His eyes squinted closed. The tequila must have burned going down. It cost him his voice for a moment. "*I* don't know who killed Sellers. *I* didn't have anything to lose, see, because we were all going to have to come up with a share of the five mill, and *I* didn't have the money in the first place. Can't wring blood from a freaking turnip."

Isobel shivered. She had no reason to disbelieve his story. And if it was true, then Gina Sellers had been playing both ends against the middle. Extorting money from the legitimate Candless heirs on the one hand, against the threat of accepting Ian's offer, and agreeing to accept the offer anyway in exchange for the protection and money the Feds had offered her.

Where had a fresh-faced girl from Utah come up with such a plan, or such nerves of steel?

"I don't want your money, Harrison. Or anyone else's. You can report back to whoever put you up to this that I didn't just rush in to take up where Gina left off."

"You intend to stay here and be the kid's nanny?"

"Yes." She had no intention at all of staying here, where Candless could work his disastrous influence on Seth, but saying as much was out of the question. She had to appear, for the sake of the government investigation, to want nothing more than to be employed as Seth's nanny for as long as she could. She gave him a curious look she had to conjure up. "Is that so hard to believe?"

He stared at her. "Are you really that freaking stupid?"

Dear God, where was he going with this? Shouldn't it have eased his mind that she had planned no extortion?

"Do you think," he went on, "that we want his bastard brat or you hanging around here? Lady, you *are* too dumb to live." He reached for the gun, picked it up and aimed the barrel straight at her forehead. "Let's just see how dumb luck holds up."

Her throat closed off, her mouth pooled with saliva. He could not afford the extortion, but he could afford to lose his inheritance to Seth even less. He must be too drunk to judge his actions. She had none of her angel powers left, save some residual ability to slow time in her mind.

She saw his fingers curling tighter around the grip, the alcohol clouding his senses, the hesitation, maybe the stray thought occurring to him that to put a bullet through her head here in the kitchen of his father's guarded estate would be the truly stupid thing to do.

"Don't do it, Harrison. Don't do it."

"Shut up!" Through his anger and all the betrayal he had ever suffered at his father's whim, the tequila won out. "Just shut up!" He swallowed. "You're not stupid at all, are you?" he shouted. "You're just holding out for more!"

Nothing she could say would convince him otherwise. She let her hands trail off the edge of the table. His forefinger began to squeeze the trigger.

Her heart skipped a beat. Seth filled her mind. Another beat. Angelo…dear God.

A third. She would not go down, not if she could help it. She had only this life, and no one was going to take it from her, not now.

She butted her hands against the table's edge. If she could lift it high enough, shove it hard enough, she could deflect his aim, topple him over. But the table was too heavy, and in the split second she saw his finger jerk back, adrenaline poured through her as the trigger clicked and the hammer slammed home.

Chapter Ten

In the silence afterwards, after the trigger clicking, after the bullet which was in the proper groove to fire failed, Isobel came undone.

Harrison Candless lay slumped on the table as if he had been shot, and Angelo stood, wrathful and glorious, powerful and angry, stretching out an arm toward Harrison as if he were Moses parting the Red Sea. The half-empty tequila bottle went dry as the wilderness, and the gun he had dared aim at Isobel withered to dust and vanished into thin air.

Relief flooded her body. Her breath came out in giant heaves. She would have thrown up if there had been anything in her stomach. She had come so close to losing everything she had defied heaven and earth to be—a living breathing woman, who desired to mother a baby who had lost his own.

She longed to fling herself into Angelo's outstretched arms, to abandon her resolve. But what she wanted most was to bathe herself in the safety and security of knowing he would be there for her no matter what happened, for so long as she lived. But that was false hope.

He had saved her life just now, but she would

spend it without him, so she sat there hugging herself, willing her shaking to cease, and wiped the tears of relief from her face. She met Angelo's angry gaze. "Is he..."

"Passed out." He straightened and lowered his arms. "If he remembers this at all, it will be in a nightmare."

By Angelo's tone, Isobel believed Harrison Candless would suffer his nightmares. He would have killed her, and still she knew inside herself the towering pain that brought him to such a brink. She wouldn't wish Angelo's vengeance upon a flea.

"He's been so wounded—"

"He's not beyond help, Iso," Angelo warned her. He would not soften his rebuke. "He is the cause of what he becomes. His nightmares will serve him well."

She stood shakily. "I want to get out of here. Is Seth by himself?"

"He is fine. Sleeping. In the charge of an army of Guardian Angels."

She nodded, relieved, and took up her teacup.

"Leave it," Angelo commanded.

"But they'll know I was here by the video—"

"The tapes will show that you were here and gone before he arrived." He gestured toward Harrison Candless with his head, but his eyes never left her. His look unnerved her for its possessiveness, for his expectation that she would do what he told her.

She didn't want to do what he said, anything he said. She wouldn't be at his beck and call, at his whim or command in even so trivial a matter, even if he had saved her life. She turned away with the cup. "I'd rather wash it and put it away."

He came as close to swearing then as he had ever come. He had had it up to his mortal-seeming eyeballs with Pascal and his marriage-of-convenience accusation, and he didn't need Isobel behaving like this.

She thought she had come too close. It could never happen. He would defend her to the ends of the earth, so that if he chose, she would never die. But the all-too-human panic that had consumed him in the instant of what she perceived to be the greatest danger still pounded through his being. He was scared and angry, and he hadn't been scared in a very long time.

He took the cup and saucer from her, shut off the water, made it clean and replaced it in the glass-fronted cabinets long before she could begin to offer a protest.

"Let's go."

"Fine." She turned from him and went through the door, pulling it shut behind her.

He simply went through door, the physical matter meaning nothing to him. He meant to keep stoking his anger, but it guttered out. "Isobel, stop."

"Or what?" She kept on walking. "I've been through too much tonight to deal with you anymore, Angelo." Her voice came perilously close to cracking with tears. "You saved my life, but you don't own me. I won't put up with your attitude anymore. I loved you once, but—"

"Don't say it...Iso," he pleaded, more desperate now than if he had his own human emotions.

"Don't tell me what to say or not to say, Angelo! You have *no* say over me. You don't love me—"

"That's not true—"

"—nor are you still the man I loved. Or else I was

crazy. You need to get out. Send your Rafe Santini or Pascal, or let Pascal send someone else.''

When had he ever even spoken Pascal's name to her? What had he done? ''Iso, I'm begging you—''

''Don't,'' she cried, whirling on him. ''I mean it, Angelo. Damn you, I mean it! I can't do this anymore!''

''Neither can I, Iso.'' He choked. What moonlight there was sparkled in her unspent tears. What hope there was rankled in his heart, mocking him for a fool of an angel. Was he too late, had he turned her away one time too many? ''I can't be with you and not...love you.''

She froze as if he had physically caused her to do so. She swallowed. Her chin dipped low and she dashed away her tears. She stood there in her pretty little dress with all its tiny buttons and the skirt lifting in the breeze about her thighs, her breasts heaving, her arms empty, her hands clenched tight. She searched his eyes, his face, his being, not trusting what she had heard or what it meant.

Not trusting herself, he knew, to judge correctly. Her naked confusion plucked at his soul.

''Iso, it's true.'' He moved toward her because he could do nothing else. In his mind he begged her to stay still. ''I can't...not...be with you. I swear to you it's true.''

She moved toward him. He wanted to think it was because she had lied, that she had no real desire to be apart from him.

''You're certain,'' she whispered, anxious about the babe, ''that Seth is safe?''

''I promised you, Iso. Nothing will happen to him. He is protected.''

Reassured, she let him take her in his arms and he gained hope.

She let him draw her body tightly to his, and he began to believe.

She let him bring her closer, his hand cupping her bottom, let herself feel his passion risen against her, let herself cry out and go moist and cry out again, this time crying *his name*. Then he knew for God's own truth that his making love with Isobel Avedon was more sacred in heaven and on earth than avenging all the evils the world had ever known.

He gave himself to her. He lifted her so that her legs encircled his waist and he could feel her heat. He buried his face in her swollen breasts and began to turn, and turn, and turn until they were no longer halfway between the kitchen and Seth's nursery suite, but on the beach, on a blanket of the finest mohair, beneath the full moon from which all the clouds had, at his will, blown away.

He laid her down on the blanket and covered her body with his, her lips with his. Her heart and soul with his. He held her face cupped reverently in his hands, and kissed her till he knew for certain that there was no elixir, no honey, no wine more heady and earthy and sweet than her lips.

His member throbbed, his heart soared. Isobel pulled his shirt from his jeans and let her hands move beneath the soft denim to thread her fingers in the mass of his dark and curling chest hair. Her fingers touched his nipples, her pleasured murmur filled his mouth.

His excitement pitched out of sight and mind. Angelo de Medici was a virgin. He had waited five hundred years for this.

For this.

But though he wished to bury himself inside her, to go inside where he longed to be, to go *home,* he took his time with her. Isobel was a virgin as well.

"I love you, Iso. I love you." He kissed her neck and touched his lips to the tops of her tender breasts, then raised up for her to undo her own buttons and his. His throat thickened, for in the moonlight the moisture beading on her nipples reminded him how thick his member had grown after she'd taken the babe from her breast and he'd caught a glimpse of her, damp and puckered and flushed in her cheeks with a profound and womanly maternal pleasure.

She represented to him everything a mortal woman could be—feminine, sensual, sensitive, heartful, maternal. Sexual.

He touched his tongue to her beaded breast, his hand to the dark moist cavity between her legs, and Isobel simply dissolved in pleasure.

His desire for her unraveled whatever hesitation, whatever fear she had left inside her. He had made his choice and he had made it for her. Whether he went back now to the corps of Avenging Angels or never did, he had chosen once for her.

The ocean sucked gently at wet shifting sands glistening in the moonlight, blurring the boundaries between earth and sea, drawing one into the other, giving and taking, tide pools spilling free and sinking deeper for it, to hold more, still more.

An echo, she thought.

An echo of their lovemaking, repeating itself endlessly. She went willingly to him and opened herself and came, then came again with the touch of his fingers, before he finally entered her. And thus, they entered eternity together.

THEY SAT SPOONED TOGETHER inside the blanket, Angelo with his back to the cliff side, Isobel between his legs, her back against his chest. They stayed that way until the moon set.

She pulled away to dress when her breasts began to ache severely.

"Tell me what it's like, Iso, when it hurts." He didn't want her to hurt.

She groaned and shoved his hands away as playfully as she could for a woman whose babe needed his breakfast. Badly. "Your skin is hot and tight, you feel like you're going to burst. You feel like if something doesn't happen, and soon, you'll go mad." She pulled her dress over her head and began to do up the buttons. "Think about it."

He didn't have to. He grinned as if he'd learned it from the devil himself. "That good, huh?"

"That good," she answered, blushing red as a firebush in fall, then headed for the staircase built into the cliff. "Step on it, mister, 'cause I'm out of here."

He pulled on his jeans and shirt and followed. He'd known sweeter moments, but none so recklessly joyful as teasing her. He held back so he could watch the stiff morning sea breezes whip her skirt tight against her slender legs. This was lust, no doubt, but lust in the service of feelings so deep for her that to consider it a sin would be a worse sin. But now she needed, he knew, to return to the babe and ease her needless fears.

He walked with her through the hedges and fragrant flowers and the earliest sun rays over the horizon, and when she had changed Seth, settled into the sofa and taken him to her breast, she became practical again and asked whether Angelo had heard all of her encounter with Harrison Candless.

He had.

She shook her head. "I was prepared to believe that someone in this family was willing to go to any lengths to take Seth out of the picture, but I guess I would rather have believed that Gina's murder was a random act of violence."

"Or that her death had something to do with her willingness to work with the strike force? That is still possible. But you knew, Iso," he chided gently. "You had to know that once Ian Candless acknowledged Seth as his son, killing Gina and Seth was the most expedient and permanent way to solve the problem of another heir."

"Gina must have seen it coming."

"I agree. She had to have hoped that before that could happen, the Candless heirs would pay her to disappear and take Seth out of the picture with her."

"How could they ever be sure she wouldn't come back for more?"

"They couldn't. But if you were Gina, and you believed the legitimate Candless heirs would kill you anyway, you'd have nothing to lose by asking, and everything to gain. Whatever money Gina could extort from them would have given her the means to disappear. What would you do?"

"I wouldn't have thought to extort money in the first place."

"But if it were you, Iso?"

"Then—remember, this is not me—but if I had been in Gina's position, I would have taken the money and given the baby up for a private adoption.''

"You're right. That's nothing Gina would have thought of. But look at the cost benefit of proceeding with a murder. If the Candless heirs hired a hit and something went wrong, and something almost always goes wrong, one or all of them could wind up going to prison. On the other hand, if they paid Gina off, the worst-case scenario is pretty benign. They claim they were only doing what was right by Gina, compensating her for Seth's care and the damage their father had done her reputation.''

"Except Harrison, for one, didn't have his share of the money. Do you know anything about the rest, whether Conrad or Bruce or Kelsey had that kind of money lying around?''

"The only one who's independent of IJ Candless & Sons is Bruce. I've heard him wheeling and dealing with his broker, and, of course, he owns a construction company that has government contracts all over the country for low-income housing.''

Isobel had seen a feature in the newspaper a few days ago that held Bruce Candless up as a media darling and colleague of several mayors. They all sang his praises as being one of the visionaries of his generation, making a real difference in the inner cities.

"Are you saying he could have gotten his hands on his share of Gina's payoff demand?''

"He's the only one who could have done it without some fancy explaining to Candless's suits.''

"Suits?''

"Money changers, Iso,'' he teased. She rolled her eyes. He loved the flash of silvery blue, the shape of her eyebrows. The curve of her lips. His own mouth went dry to think how much he loved her, craved her. He cleared his desert-dry throat. "The guys who really control the family fortune."

A tiny vertical furrow shaped itself in her forehead just over her nose. She was not immune to the vibes of intimacy passing between them, but she wanted to understand. "Okay. The heirs had a problem. If they could come up with the money, they could get rid of Gina and Seth, but they couldn't easily lay their hands on the amount she asked. Would Bruce have covered for them all? Or would they have come back to Gina and offered less?"

"My instinct tells me Bruce had no interest in covering them."

"Really? Why not? He's the one who's always smoothing things over, always getting Candless off their cases."

"What does that prove, Iso? That he's a good guy, or that he's only a good guy when it's easy? He's smart, he's made it on his own, he's kind to his mother and he stands up for his siblings. But the kind of man he is doesn't suffer fools well, Iso, and I think he's suffered them about as much as he ever will."

"Are they such fools, Angelo?"

"When you're an adult and you depend on your father for your next meal or your next Porsche, you're a fool."

"I don't understand. Have you seen or heard Bruce treat any of them that way?"

He shook his head. "Not even once. I told you, this is my instinct."

"Have you ever been wrong?"

"No." He gave a lazy smile. "But it could happen."

"You truly are insufferable."

But her own smile matched his. Seth grinned up at her with her nipple still in his mouth, and her smile widened. "You think that's funny, little mister?" she scolded with nothing but love in her voice.

The image could not have been any less provocative, and still Angelo's sex thickened. More than her smile or her voice, more than her touch, the things most powerfully feminine about her were what drew him like the thornbird to its death.

And he had died out there on the beach in the night, there could be no question. Died to everything he knew, everything he had been since the night he watched his murderers murder Isobel first.

"Angelo, what is it?"

The alarm in her voice rattled him. "What?"

"You looked as if you'd seen a ghost—I mean, as if you'd—Angelo, what? What is it? Please tell me."

He had seen a ghost, seen her spirit leave her body, seen her body fall to the ground, her life's blood dripping from the blade of a sword he knew too well.

"There's no point, Iso."

"But there must be, or you wouldn't be so pale..."

He supposed there was no point, either, in keeping the truth from her. He had heard the sentiment she had not spoken the night before, that she would not want his vengeance visited upon a flea. He swallowed hard, cleared his throat. "That night, Iso, the night you believed me dead, I did not die. I didn't wake for three days, the morning of the day you were murdered, but I survived that long."

"Oh, God, Angelo. I'm sorry. I didn't know."

All she could think of, he could see, was how he must have suffered. That was the way her soul worked, the natural contour of her thoughts. Just as with Harrison Candless, she looked first for the suffering and, thereafter, discounted the danger, or the evil, or the malignant intentions.

She was a hopeless romantic, in his never humble opinion, as relentlessly mired in compassion as he was in his quest for justice. But then, she had not been kept alive for the express purpose of watching him die.

"Stow your compassion, Iso, and listen to me!" he railed, returning his thoughts to that night five hundred years before. "The bastards planned your murder all along."

She paled at that, but then shook off her dread. "Angelo, what does it matter now? Why torment yourself with such memories?"

"I have no choice, Iso." He dragged a hand through his hair, which hung loose from its usual thong. Why had the memories risen in him so strongly now? "The memories come upon me. There's a lesson in them. Feel it," he urged her. "There's power in knowing the truth."

Seth had finished nursing. She sat him up in her lap and patted his back. "Go on with it then, *mi amor*."

He took a deep breath, touched deeply not only by her care of Seth, but also by her endearment. He rose and began to pace like a leopard suddenly caged.

"When he learned that I had not died instantly, my distant cousin, the Pope, commanded I be kept alive. My arms and legs were broken. My eyes were all but swelled shut. I blacked out if I so much as tried to get to my hands and knees.''

He was scaring her, he knew, but he felt compelled to continue, knew that if he could just get it out, she would see if there was some point he had missed all these centuries, or, at the very least, understand how and why he had become what he had. "I didn't die that night or the next. They spared no effort keeping me alive. I would die sooner or later, and if later, then I should learn before I went to my Maker what happens to a man who dared defy their little reign of terror.''

Her palm rubbing small desperate circles on Seth's back, Isobel's eyes glittered with tears. She had lived through the religious and political intrigues herself, and still could not fathom the hidden agendas, the power struggles, and most especially not the murders. "I don't understand.''

He swallowed. He relived the hours in an instant, all its gore and the stench of his own bloodied body. "I'm not even sure I could see from both eyes, but they kept me alive so that I might have the privilege of watching you murdered.''

"To what end?'' she cried softly, clinging to the babe.

"So I might know that I was…'' he stopped, his voice thick with emotion, "powerless to stop them. Or even afterward, to avenge your death.''

Sickened, she could find no words at all, none of consolation or even comprehension. Such vile intentions were outside her realm of thinking. Her throat ached with sorrow. "What happened then?''

"I died. I was conscripted to the Avenging Angels, and I believed that was why, because vengeance was denied me in life. Because I had become vengeance incarnate, and there was so much evil to counter." He paced toward the French doors and stood watching outside, the color of the ocean, the turmoil, the swoop of gulls. "I was good. I was the best." His head hung low to hear himself making such a claim. He could hear his own arrogance, his own proud and overweening attitude. "I *am* the best."

"But you are not at peace."

He looked to Isobel and saw in her eyes the sudden and terrifyingly simple insight that in heaven and earth and hell combined, the most tortured souls belonged to the Avenging Angels.

HARRISON, THEY SUSPECTED, would not be the only one to approach Isobel. If he expected to be blackmailed by her, then the others must as well. But none of them came around the following morning, which was Sunday. By lunchtime, none of the family had yet made appearances. Helena brought word that Ian Candless wished to see his son and speak with Isobel privately at one-thirty.

She instructed Helena to tell Mr. Candless that she would be taking the baby outdoors then, and would see him on the lawn.

From her vantage point on the grassy bluff high above the sea, she could see the sliver of beach where Angelo had made love to her. The visual memory provoked others more starkly drawn, of his hands cupping her, his brow furrowing in the sweet release of their lovemaking, the taste of his tears, the thump of his heart close to hers.

He sat there now, his broad naked back to her, his hair pulled back into the leather thong, his attention at once on the hypnotic waves and, from a higher perspective, on her. He would hear every word that passed between her and Candless. He would be contemplating, she knew, what meaning there was to his existence after their coupling the night before.

She couldn't fathom how this might turn out. He had served the role of avenger for so long, and for such powerful, personal reasons, that he knew nothing else. He didn't even recognize peace where he found it—in her embrace.

Isobel shivered and drew her attention back to Seth. She spread a pillowy dark plaid comforter on the grass near a stone bench a short distance from the cliff side, then placed the babe in the midst with a menagerie of small stuffed animals. Seth favored the armadillo, whose snout went constantly into his mouth.

Her heart, as it did in such moments, swelled with wonder. Were he one of Raphael's beautiful blond cherubs, she could not have loved Seth more. The tiny dimples in his chubby little hands brought her to some indefinable brink of emotion. His toothless smile took her breath straight away. His babbling was a symphony to her ears, his struggles to match the wobbly movement of his arms and legs in an effort to crawl, a feast for her eyes.

After a few more attempts, he gave up with a frustrated cry and rolled onto his back. Bending over him, Isobel crooned softly, gave him the consolation of a kiss and his armadillo, then sat with her legs tucked to her side. She took her needlepoint in hand, absently working stitches, and waited for Ian Candless to make his appearance, wondering what he knew of Harrison's behavior last night.

Candless arrived, as always, on the stroke of the appointed time. Feeling the level of Angelo's attention to her rising, she looked up as Candless's shadow approached, shading her own eyes. He was not, however, alone. His son-in-law, Kelsey's husband, "Sinjin," the family legal counsel, accompanied him. Isobel took a deep breath and gave a greeting. "Mr. Candless. Mr. St. John."

The attorney merely nodded. Candless replied. "Good morning, Isobel. And how is my sweet boy this morning? Happy as a little lark, I see." He turned his gaze on Isobel.

She smiled and scraped together a neutral reply. "He's happy by nature, I think."

"And what of you, my dear?" Candless bent to lift the babe into his arms, while Sinjin remained carefully distant. "Have you any concerns thus far?"

Candless's tone was absolutely solicitous, interested, and...smarmy. She would rather have demanded what on God's green earth Ian Candless had been thinking to have done what he did to Harrison that Easter morning of 1977 on his son's seventh birthday. She held her tongue on that issue, let her gaze flick over the attorney, and broached the larger issue, the one for which she had come here.

"I am concerned," she said softly, watching him thrill Seth by gently tossing him in the air. "I have seen in the news that you are under a great deal of pressure."

"The issue of the exploitation of illegal immigrants?" He saw that was what she meant, and laughed, taking Seth's tiny, exploring fingers from his mouth. "A tempest in a teapot, don't you agree, Sinjin?" His son-in-law nodded. Candless went on.

"Compared to the stories we released to the press earlier this week, of your rescuing Seth and restoring him to me, such allegations are meaningless. Don't let them concern you at all."

She would not be patted on the head in such a manner. "Meaningless, sir…but are they true?"

"No." He sat on the stone bench, bouncing Seth on his knee. Isobel had to turn slightly to face him. Sinjin stood stiffly, a packet of papers under his arm, but Candless seemed, if anything, untouched by the hints of furor set off in the media over the alleged exploitation of illegal immigrant labor by Candless Industries. Curious, maybe even vaguely suspicious of her interest, but without a trace of concern.

"Even if the allegations were true," he said, patting Seth's cheek with his own tiny fist, "I would owe you no explanation. You are my son's nanny, nothing more. But I will tell you this once, and then it will be put to rest. I have never resorted to illegal practices, less than humane management, sweatshops in the Orient or importing cheap labor."

Sinjin added, "Ian's business ethics are of the highest order. He employs the handicapped. He employs design geniuses. He supports the business community and, for all this, IJ Candless & Sons has become an international success."

"The kind of success," Candless concluded, "that will inevitably become the target of scurrilous rumors."

"Inevitably?" she echoed doubtfully, thinking how deep-seated must be the belief he had branded into his youngest son. *Only the paranoid survive.*

He laughed again, not unpleasantly. "Perhaps not," he granted. "But success brings with it certain risks." He gave her a curious look. "You don't think very much of me, do you, Isobel?"

She lowered her head a moment to think. Her heart skipped beats. Instinctively, she knew his respect hinged on the same willingness to be straightforward that she had demonstrated at their first meeting. But she had not been truthful by half then, nor could she be now.

"It's true," she admitted, "that I don't approve of what happened between you and Gina Sellers. In my mind, it is adultery. Could you be less than honorable in one portion of your life, and not have such dishonor seep into your business affairs?"

"Or conversely, poison my baby son with my dishonorable conduct?"

Isobel swallowed hard. He had effectively ducked the question of his business affairs and, in doing so, cut straight to the heart of her own concern. She was trapped there now, outwitted by him, constrained from any further questions into allegations of labor exploitation against IJ Candless & Sons. She was the nanny, and her only proper concerns were for Seth's welfare.

"Yes." She kept her response that unelaborate.

He pulled Seth to his feet on his knee, supporting the wobbling baby beneath his arms. Seth loved to stand, to stiffen his little legs and stretch his torso high. Candless appeared entranced for a moment, unable to take his eyes off Seth's small triumph. But when he looked at Isobel again, his eyes reflected a good deal less than someone entranced, and when he spoke, it had nothing to do with his lack of honor poisoning his son.

"It's obvious to us all, Isobel, that you have fallen hook, line and sinker for my son."

Alarm skittered across her nerves at the realization that he saw how attached, how in love with this baby she was. It gave him a certain power over her. Control. He had only to threaten to remove her in order to make her toe his line, and despite the kind words, she saw that he intended just such a message.

This, she thought, was the pressure, the subtle coercion, the bullying nature that Harrison and his siblings, even Candless's wife Patrice, must have suffered.

Maybe Isobel was being unfair to Ian Candless. It was obvious to her by the way he took the baby up and gently tossed him in the air, by the way he buried his nose in the babe's neck, by the way he looked at his son, searching Seth's face for features, expressions he could call his own, that he doted on the babe.

She wanted to understand Candless. Her natural bent, to find that one redeeming quality, persisted.

But she had only to remember his adultery and feel the same withering control over herself that he had inflicted on his adult children, for her compassion to fade into oblivion.

Making her gaze strong and sure, she agreed that what he had said was true. "I am enamored of your son, Mr. Candless. I couldn't love him more if he were my own."

"Well, you see, that's a little troubling. He is not your son."

Where was he going with this? "I know that."

"But you would not think of trying to steal my son away."

She fought off the shiver that possessed her. "I—"

"Because, you see," he interrupted her, tossing Seth gently into the air, his tone anything but gentle, "my son Bruce came to me this morning with tales of Harry blubbering in the night."

He paused. Isobel's heart all but stopped.

He tossed Seth into the air again. The baby squealed in delight. Isobel cringed at the distance Seth fell before his father plucked him from the air.

"And what do you suppose the blubbering was about?" Candless queried.

"I—"

"Don't trouble yourself inventing a lie, Ms. Avedon. Bruce confessed to me that Seth's mother attempted a shameless extortion. It now seems sweet Harry is wildly asserting that you are of a like mind."

Chapter Eleven

Isobel's heart knocked painfully beneath her ribs. Why hadn't Angelo known this?...but, of course, they had been making love on the beach when Harry must have gone to see Bruce. And later, when Bruce took the story to his father, Angelo was finally admitting to her that he had survived to see her death. And why it was that his vengeance was so fierce she would not want it visited upon a flea.

In the instant she understood what had happened, Angelo materialized, visible only to her, behind Ian Candless and Sinjin. He had heard the conversation in every detail, and Isobel suspected he knew, as well, her desperate train of thoughts.

She thought it would have been a fine time to create a small time warp, to give her time to think how she should respond. Angelo, apparently, did not.

"Just defend yourself, Iso," he warned. "Anyone would be flustered. They expect it."

Aware of Sinjin studying her, Isobel met Candless's granite-hard stare straight on. "Harrison is mistaken."

"Am I to take your word over my son's?"

"As to my intentions, yes."

"Why would Harry invent such a wild-eyed tale?"

"I don't suppose he invented all of it, if Gina made such demands." The truth was that Harrison Candless lived a paranoid existence, and that his father had instilled that brand of craziness in his son at an early age. With less at stake, she would have called Ian Candless on his own responsibility. Instead, she tempered her response. "Harrison's fears of me are groundless. He is mistaken if he believes I came here with any thought of blackmail."

"Yet we have not discussed the matter of your compensation."

Was he saying that he didn't believe her? Isobel met Angelo's eyes. To Candless and his son-in-law, she must have appeared to be staring off into space.

"He's nervous, Iso," Angelo said softly. "He can't fathom your purpose in saving Seth's life. He is deeply skeptical, paranoid. St. John has almost certainly insisted that you are not to be trusted. That you have some other agenda."

Isobel took a deep breath. She had scolded Angelo days ago for thinking her naive. She wasn't. She knew the evil that existed, had known it from the moment Angelo's own jackbooted brother had struck him a killing blow. And still, *still*, most of the time she forgot to think what ulterior motives moved in the hearts of human beings.

She had none herself, but she'd better learn—and learn fast—to look at reality with open eyes.

Angelo approved her resolve. "The only thing Candless wants is to be reassured that you were not connected with Gina, and that you knew nothing about any plan to extort money from the heirs. Remember, you know none of this. Wait them out. Even now he has other reasons for having this conversation with you. Just keep to your line.''

The exchange between them had taken no real time. She brought her focus back to her employer. ''Mr. Candless, you offered me anything I desired in exchange for returning your son. If I had wanted money—any amount of money—wouldn't I have simply taken it then? Or if I had wanted to steal Seth from you, why would I have even come forward?''

''That's where you become disingenuous, Ms. Avedon,'' Sinjin charged. ''It takes money to disappear—and get away with it. You know Mr. Candless would have tracked you to the ends of the earth. He would have given you almost any amount of money, but never his son. You could not have both Seth and the amount of money necessary to pull off a clean escape without following in Gina's footsteps.''

Isobel tilted her head. Something in Candless's expression, in his manner, in the way he eyed his son-in-law, betrayed Sinjin's charges. The attorney clearly believed in the possibilities he spouted, but Candless? Nearly certain that she was being manipulated, that Candless was the disingenuous one, that he was toying with both her and St. John, she took another deep breath and saw that it was true.

Ian Candless had not entertained the notion for very long at all that she had ever intended to carry out Gina's plan on her own behalf—which could only mean he had set up this encounter to toss a gauntlet at the feet of St. John.

Angelo nodded slowly. ''I agree, Iso. You're not the target at the moment.''

Playing peekaboo with Seth as he sat on Candless's lap, she braced herself. "Mr. Candless, why don't you just say what you want from me?"

"You see, Sinjin? Our Ms. Avedon is nothing if not straightforward." He gave a great, hearty belly laugh. Startled, Seth began to whimper. "Oh, what is it, wee one?" Candless crooned, handing him over to Isobel. "I couldn't be sure, you know," he said to her. "I had your references checked. I knew you were exactly what you claimed to be—"

"Perhaps too perfectly what you claimed," Sinjin interrupted.

Angelo had every base covered, but of course neither Candless nor St. John could imagine that Isobel was none of what she claimed. She said nothing, knowing there was nothing she could say that wasn't a half-truth of its own. Angelo stood silently by, approving her silence.

It didn't matter. The real clash was going on between Candless and Sinjin. "Perhaps," he mused, coming to the point of the charade he had created here, "it is the other way about." He turned sharply on his son-in-law. "Perhaps it is you, Sinjin, and the others, my devoted children, who are so willing to be rid of another heir as to imagine Isobel would take such a bribe."

A weaker man would have crumbled under Candless's pointed accusation. Unfazed, comfortable against all odds, St. John shook his head. "I warned you, Ian, that bringing Seth into this household would crack the family wide open. You have no one but yourself to blame for inflaming the insecurities of your legitimate heirs. What's more, you know it."

Candless turned away, toward Isobel, his back to

Sinjin. "You cannot begin to imagine, Isobel, the ways in which the specter of money will change people. A fender bender becomes cause for a multimillion-dollar lawsuit. A disgruntled employee blows the whistle, seeking damages for God alone knows what."

Was he expecting her to sympathize with the plight of the wealthy, the unpleasant realities that made them the targets of the greedy poor, or was he merely trying to justify his own paranoia?

He looked from Emory St. John to Isobel and back again, then went on. "Of course, I am certain I will never find that my son-in-law and legal counsel has been less than loyal to me. Or that you are anything other than a nanny who's simply head over heels about my son. Forgive me. I had to ask."

Then he left, and St. John stayed. She watched the clothing magnate cross the rolling, manicured lawn until he disappeared from sight.

Candless's show of asking her forgiveness took nothing away from Isobel's anger. A part of her berated herself. She was, after all, in his home and in the bosom of his family under still falser pretenses than even he had begun to suspect. But Ian Candless's manipulation—the subtle clubbing, the threat underlying his certainty that he would never find her more or less than she claimed to be—made her blood boil. This was the tyranny that Bruce, Conrad, Harrison and Kelsey had grown up with, that his wife must inevitably have suffered over the years.

Laying Seth on his tummy with the beloved armadillo, she turned to St. John, who remained seated on the stone bench watching her.

He crossed his arms over his chest. "I expect we're all a bit more than you bargained for."

"I didn't know what to expect," she replied. "And the only bargain I wanted was to take care of this baby."

Sinjin's eyes narrowed, following in the direction of his father-in-law's departure. "He didn't tell you the rest of Harry's wild tale. Did he have a gun when he confronted you last night?"

Isobel nodded. "Only one bullet though." Sinjin laughed shortly. Though she had made a joke, the subject wasn't funny and he apparently sensed that she didn't take it lightly. "I went to the kitchen to brew a cup a tea. I found him there with his gun and a bottle of tequila. To be fair to Harrison, it's not as if he came looking for me with murder on his mind."

"Do you believe he meant to harm himself, that he was playing some twisted game of Russian roulette?"

Isobel shrugged. "I don't know. The bullet wasn't even in the gun when I first arrived. He seemed consumed with guilt."

"Guilt?" Sinjin looked at his hands. "Over what?"

"Maybe you can tell me."

He scowled deeply. Behind him, Angelo laughed softly. "I don't like games, Ms. Avedon."

"I love games, Mr. St. John, but not this sort. I feel as if I've come late to the party, into the middle of some truth-or-dare match where the stakes involve Seth's life."

St. John laughed unpleasantly. "*Truth*-or-dare would not be an accurate description. The truth tends to be buried in this family, only to be dragged up when the corpse is rotting.''

Isobel shuddered inside at his graphic confession. Every instinct in her wanted to snatch Seth up from the blanket and run as fast and as far as she could. She had to make herself sit there, touching the babe, reassuring herself that this minute, at least, the baby was not in any danger. She had a dozen or more questions. Perhaps Sinjin was in a mood to answer some of them.

''Is it true that Gina attempted to blackmail Harrison and the others?''

He shrugged as if he'd had no prior knowledge of this. ''I believe Bruce. Harry's a bit off the wall.''

''What about Kelsey? You would know if your wife—''

''If she were about to pay off a blackmailer?'' he interrupted. ''I would be the last person to know what my wife was doing.'' He grimaced. ''Kelsey is devious in the extreme. If it came to a question of my opinion or Conrad's—even Bruce's—opinion of her, she would inevitably choose her brothers' regard. Don't get me wrong, Isobel. I love my wife, all the more, perhaps, for her familial foibles. Patrice refers to this as my particular Achilles' heel.''

''Patrice? Does she think so little of her own daughter?''

St. John sighed heavily. ''Let us simply say that Patrice has no illusions as to the shortcomings of her children.''

She began to reply, when Angelo suggested, ''Ask again, Iso, if it can possibly be true that he knew nothing of Gina's blackmail—or if Candless was on the right track.''

She studied her hands a moment, feeling inexplicably nervous about challenging St. John. Angelo gave her a nod. She straightened her shoulders.

"Sinjin, I don't believe it's possible that you didn't know what Gina was up to. Was he right just now?" she asked, angling her head in the direction Candless had taken. "Was it the heirs offering a bribe and not Gina demanding extortion money?" Her voice came out more softly, with less certainty than she wanted. Maybe, though, it was more nannylike, maybe safer with a shark like Emory St. John, than if she'd managed to sound more assured.

He gave her a sharp look nevertheless, then took a deep breath and sent his gaze far out onto the horizon of the glittering ocean. After a moment, he returned his attention to her. "I have no knowledge of a bribe offered to Gina Sellers. As I started to say, Isobel, when I suggested that this family was more than you bargained for, you have no idea of the turmoil the existence of this child has caused."

Isobel swallowed hard. "Seth was meant to die along with Gina in that drive-by shooting, wasn't he?"

St. John scowled. "Again, I have no knowledge of that whatsoever."

"Then what do you mean?"

"Perhaps if I lay all the cards on the table, you can make a more…informed choice as to whether you wish to stay."

She began to protest that there was nothing he could say that would cause her to choose any option but staying with Seth. Angelo forestalled her. "Let's hear what he believes he must tell you, Iso, and then decide how to respond."

She nodded, indicating she would listen to St. John. "All right."

He gnawed a moment at the inside corner of his lip, then began. "I knew Gina Sellers fairly well—or I should say, I came to know her. After Ian was…done with her, I leased the condo for her, arranged for her to move in there, then gave her several thousand dollars to help her get on with her life."

Isobel frowned. Hadn't Kathryn Weston told them that dealing with the aftermath of Candless's affairs was his son Bruce's province?

"What is it?" Sinjin demanded.

"Nothing. I only thought Bruce had done that for Gina."

St. John gave a short, barking laugh. "Who told you that? Surely not Bruce?"

"Who else?"

He waved off the issue impatiently. "Ian was scrupulously discreet. It's true that when he got to be a certain age, Bruce came and went with his father's…liaisons. I believe he did as asked with the intention of protecting his mother from the indignity of knowing of the affairs, which is inevitable when the chauffeur knows more of your husband's whereabouts and extracurricular activities than you."

Isobel felt her stomach sour. Ian Candless's affairs galled her; his son's attempts to protect his mother were just as inevitably futile. A woman knows—Isobel believed that with all her heart. What could Bruce have been thinking? Surely his complicity had hurt Patrice almost as much as her husband's infidelities.

St. John must have read the distaste in her expression. "Ian Candless has many fine qualities. His business ethics are of the highest order. Unfortunately, loyalty to his wife isn't among his attributes."

"Or regard for his children."

"Quite true. No one knows that better than I, Isobel, I can assure you. You would have to understand the miserable circumstances from which he came in order to have even the remotest sense of what he has overcome in his life to be able to provide this kind of life-style for his family. He is, at the very least, an elegant provider."

"I'm sorry, Sinjin. I don't believe that *things* compensate for the rest."

"Which is why you are ill suited to manage here, Isobel."

On the contrary, she thought fiercely. That was why she must stay, if Seth must belong to this family. Precisely so that she could provide the precious baby the love he wouldn't get from anyone else.

St. John resumed his story. "In any case, I knew that Gina Sellers was pregnant long before her condition began to show. She told me herself. She indicated to me that she was several weeks along—as many as twelve or sixteen. I knew the date of her first encounter with Ian, which was only seven weeks prior to our discussion. Ian could not be the father. She wanted to go back to Utah after the baby was born. I told her that I would see to it that once her lease was up and the baby was born, she would have the necessary money to relocate."

Isobel's heart thumped. "If Seth isn't his—"

"She lied."

"She lied? To you? Why would she do that? Why wouldn't she tell you Seth was Candless's baby from the start?"

He shook his head. "I wish I knew. The only reasonable explanation I can come up with is that she wanted to keep her options open. If she confessed too early that the baby was Ian's, she would close off any other avenues she might have had."

Angelo whistled softly. The baby, who could also hear him, grinned and turned toward the sound. Isobel sat stunned. "That could only be true if Gina assumed Candless would want Seth!"

"Nonetheless, Isobel, it is what it is. Trust me on this. It was the first of a couple of nasty surprises to me."

She shook her head. "I don't understand."

"Allow me to explain. It was only after Seth was born, in fact three *months* later, when the lease on the condo was set to expire, that she told me Seth was Ian's son. That she was afraid to say so earlier. Naturally, I didn't believe her. She had told me how far along she was in the beginning, and there was no way Ian could have been the father."

"What did you do?"

"I arranged for paternity testing. Ian was ecstatic at the possibility—the first of the nasty surprises to me—but I thought little of it. However thrilled he was at the prospect of an infant son, nothing would come of it. I knew he could not be the father."

"But the paternity testing proved that he was?"

"Imagine my surprise." St. John snorted. "I had hired the most reputable lab in the country. There could be no dispute. Seth was, to a ninety-nine-point-nine-percent certainty, the son of Ian Candless."

Whatever hope had caused her heart to thump died in Isobel's breast. "What did you do then?"

He shrugged. "I conveyed Ian's offer to Miss Sellers. The one he spoke of on the television the night of her death."

"What did she say? What did she do?"

"She went quite pale. It would be an understatement to say she was taken off guard. I believed at the time that her reaction meant that the last thing Gina Sellers wanted was to be stuck nannying her own child, with the status of a servant, but I could have been wrong. In any case, Ian's offer was obviously not what she had been hoping for. She asked for a few days to think about how it all might work, to think, she said, what would be best for Seth."

"Did Bruce know any of this?"

St. John frowned. "Bruce?"

"Did anyone else know, for that matter?" Isobel persisted.

"I can assure you there were only three people on the planet who knew of the offer. Ian Candless, Gina Sellers, and me. Why do you ask?"

"Because if any of them—Bruce or Conrad or Harrison, or even Kelsey—knew what was up, that their father was about to claim another heir, and an illegitimate one, wouldn't that be motive enough for murder?"

St. John's features hardened. "It would. If they knew. The possibility has certainly crossed Ian's mind, especially after last night. There have been no breaks in the police investigation. He has hired his own investigators. I believe it is his intention to establish a personal bodyguard on the estate before the day is out."

"For Seth?" A chill took hold of her. She knew in that instant that Angelo himself would somehow turn up as the bodyguard hired to protect Seth. The possibility that it was one of the Candless heirs who had contracted for the murder of Seth and his mother was nothing more than she and Angelo had suspected from the start, but for Candless to believe it of his own sons and daughter?

"For Seth, of course," Sinjin confirmed. "And for you, as well." He sighed heavily. "I'd like to believe he's mad to think any of them capable of such a thing, but frankly, I don't know anymore. Another encounter like the one you had last night might not end so harmlessly."

"If no one knew, though…is it possible that your conversations with Candless were overheard?"

"No. When we spoke of these matters it was in the limousine on our way to other things, and the partition is always raised. Not even the chauffeur could have overheard. But I suppose it is possible that in some cruel, perverse moment Ian might actually have told one of the family himself."

"Then it's possible that at least one of them knew—and knew enough to want Gina and Seth dead?"

"It's possible." St. John's jaw tightened. "Harry is a loose cannon if ever there was one. Conrad…well, Conrad is an angry young man, to say the least. He will cut any corner, take any risk to stay on top. Bruce would have done anything to protect his mother from these indignities, and Kelsey… Dear God. I would not have thought it possible until she became pregnant with our child, but she is over the edge with the notion of Seth usurping her father's attentions and fortune." He paused, then returned to his original point. "So you see, Isobel, you would be well advised to simply leave. Find another family needing your services. Is it worth your life to stay?''

"My life," Isobel interrupted fiercely, taking Seth into the protection of her arms, "will have been for nothing if anything happens to this baby. I'm staying."

He shrugged. "Fair enough. You know the risks."

St. John left then, leaving with her the envelope containing her employment contract. It was only afterward that another question occurred to her, not one for St. John himself, but one that instead went to the heart of Gina's murder. Having read Isobel's mind, Angelo sat with her, nodding slowly. They were on exactly the same wavelength.

If it was true, and St. John had not been lying for his own reasons, that virtually no one but he knew of Candless's offer to Gina, how had the immigration investigators learned of it in time to make their Trojan horse pitch to Gina? Either St. John himself had tipped off the INS, or one of the family.

Rocking back and forth as she sat cuddling Seth, Isobel shook her head. The sun shone brightly. The scent of flowers everywhere mixed with the salty spray of the ocean and the vegetation washed ashore. All her senses were tuned to the real world. Still, she felt as if she were missing something essential.

"I don't get it, Angelo. Even if Candless *told* one of the family about Seth just to be cruel, who was served? Who could possibly have benefited by letting the immigration investigators in on the offer?"

"I don't know either, Iso." Angelo shook his head. His hair shone like a glossy fur in the sunlight. His face had become so dear and familiar and necessary to her again, that sometimes she could not breathe when he was around. Times when an expression took her back, or a smile took her where she'd never been. Now it was his utter concentration, the way his brow creased and the smile lines about his eyes deepened in thought.

Her heart knocked about. Seth patted her cheek, seeking her attention. She smiled for him while returning her attention to Angelo's words, putting aside how she had already come to depend on his being there, and how he might never be again when this was all done.

If he knew her thoughts, he feigned otherwise. "Remember this, though. You suspected from the minute those INS investigators, Terrence and Landau, came knocking at Gina's door, that it was because of them—or her involvement with them—that she was murdered."

For a second, Isobel relived that terrifying moment that had reminded her so graphically of Angelo's own murder, and of the power of the state and its police, and the abuses of that power. But Seth reached up and grabbed her lower teeth, drawing her from the memory. She pretended a moment to gnaw on his tiny fingers. He screamed with the sheer delight of it. She steeped herself for that brief time in the baby's joyful innocence, but she couldn't get the puzzle out of her mind.

"I can't begin to figure this out. Someone called the INS. Someone alerted them to a possibility of getting a stoolie into the Candless estate. Does that mean Candless Industries *is* exploiting illegal alien labor?"

"I would bet the farm on it, if I had one to bet. The question is whether Ian Candless is aware of it, or if Conrad, for instance, has brought in the illegal laborers without his father knowing about it."

"Why Conrad?"

"Remember, he's the one who runs labor management for Candless Industries."

"Okay. Suppose it's Conrad who's exploiting the cheap labor. Suppose he's even responsible for bringing the laborers across the border illegally. Someone else had to know about it, because someone did tip off the INS. Doesn't the whole family stand to lose if there are penalties or convictions?"

"It depends on what you mean by losing, Iso. The family fortune couldn't be touched in legal proceedings for the exploitation of illegal immigrants. Only Seth threatened the heirs in that way."

"Could it have been a disgruntled employee? Could that be why Candless went off on that tangent about the specter of money changing people?"

"What is the likelihood that one disgruntled employee looking for a way to blow the whistle would also know anything about Seth's existence?"

"I see what you mean," Isobel agreed, helping Seth balance as he wobbled on the blanket before her. "Candless might have told one of his sons or Kelsey about Seth simply to be spiteful, but no one outside the family, surely. It has to have been one of them who tipped off Landau and Terrence. But why?"

Angelo's expression hardened and his eyes narrowed, then he let his gaze wander a moment out to sea. "Think about this, Iso. Look at this scenario—and let's suppose this is all driven by Conrad."

"Because he is head of personnel and labor at Candless Industries?"

Angelo nodded. "For argument's sake, suppose you're Conrad and you're about to get exposed— nailed by immigration for illegal labor practices. Suppose that you know the Feds are sniffing around. That they'd do anything to get a stoolie into your operation, even into your own house. Suppose if you just had a little time to clean up your act, maybe get your illegal employees out of your factories and into other jobs or out of the country, there would be no case left against you or the company—so the best thing you could do would be to create some diversion to gain a little time."

Isobel began to catch a glimpse of the whole that Angelo spun, the story he wrought. "All of that makes sense. Go on."

"Now, add to that this other little melodrama with Gina and Seth—an illegitimate heir and his upstart mother," Angelo went on. "Now, not only are your illegal labor practices about to blow up in your face. Now you're faced with a family crisis as well. Your father is about to announce to the world his paternity of a bastard child, and if you know anything about the man, you know he's doing it at least as much to cut you off at the knees as because he cares about that baby."

Isobel nodded, feeling sick at heart, sick to her stomach. This part was really nothing new. From her first night here, witnessing the interactions among the family as they were introduced to Seth, she knew that Candless was using Seth as a threat, a club to be wielded over his other children's heads, and his wife's, for as long as he lived. Hot, fierce emotions clouded her mind, and she couldn't think now where this was going.

"I'm sorry. I've lost track of your story."

He gave her a bittersweet smile that managed to convey something wicked too.

"Don't say it. I don't want to hear any more about my poor, inadequate, little mortal brain stem."

He reached toward her, and though there was only his spectral form before her, nothing of any real substance, she felt the touch of his fingers, a warmth, a sparkling, suffusing tension. He looked at her with such longing that her throat simply stopped working.

"Angelo." His name was little more than a strangled cry.

"Iso, I can't do this anymore. I can't be here, and not here in the flesh. God help me, I've fought it, but—" His voice, deep as darkness before the dawn, cracked. "I don't want to fight anymore."

Tears gathered in her eyes, her chin began to quiver. She loved him so profoundly that only her overpowering love for the innocent babe on her lap could ever matter as much.

More.

She had come to life again to care for this baby, and nothing in heaven or on earth would get in the way of doing that to her best ability. Nothing. But she ducked her head, so full of emotions now that she couldn't speak, couldn't answer Angelo, couldn't let him know what flights of fancy her heart was tempted to take if he would but come to her in the flesh...and stay. She simply didn't believe he would, in the end, forsake everything he was for her.

But he knew, as he was wont to do whenever she was speechless or silent by choice. He knew.

He kissed her then, over the babe's sweet jostling head, bringing his spectral lips to her flesh ones, his human intentions to love her, his heart on his spectral sleeve, his fate very nearly sealed in a kiss that didn't really exist.

She felt it nevertheless—the desire, the heat, the longing, the promise. She pulled back, afraid not to, equally afraid to go where this would lead before he could make this decision. They must first unravel all the twisted family intrigues that had, in all likelihood, led straight to Gina Sellers's murder.

"Are you going to somehow arrange to be the bodyguard hired for Seth?"

"It is already done, Iso. In a little while, I'll leave and arrive back here as the bodyguard from the agency that handles the estate security."

"And then you will be…flesh?"

He nodded. "But not without my powers."

It was not the absence of his angelic powers she feared, but the powers of a human male who owned her heart and soul. If he should change his mind—

"I won't…change, Iso. I can't."

She straightened. She would only believe it was true when it was true, when…if he ever gave up his angelic powers, and all the responsibility that had defined him for five hundred years.

"Please. Finish your story. How do the two problems collide, the illegal immigrants and Gina Sellers's death?"

He sat back. He would have to be content with her faith, until he made his decision known in heaven. He set aside the issues of his immortal heart and returned to her question, to his story.

"The heirs had two problems, Iso," he recapped. "One or all of them, depending on who knew about the illegal labor pool, but certainly Conrad. This couldn't have gone on without his explicit knowledge and support. So I think we can take Conrad's involvement for granted. And then Seth came into the picture. Conrad needed the time to make the labor problems go away. He needed a diversion, and they all needed to be rid of Gina Sellers and her bastard baby."

"You're assuming one or all of them heard about Seth from their father?"

"If one of them knew, all of them did, Iso."

"And are you saying Gina's murder was their solution to both problems?"

"It makes sense when you think about who it is that's in jail, charged with Gina's murder."

"The illegal immigrants..." Isobel shuddered in dismay. "Dear God. The Candless heirs set Gina up to be murdered, didn't they?"

Chapter Twelve

Angelo nodded grimly. "Someone did. The only ones with any more at stake than the heirs were the illegal immigrants themselves. They are always the ones with everything to lose. Think about this, Iso. We know it was illegal immigrants who pulled off that drive-by shooting. What would motivate them to murder Gina?"

"They had to believe she was somehow going to expose their illegal status to the INS."

"Exactly. It wouldn't be hard to make them believe she was the root of all their troubles. And what else were they going to do? They were still illegal aliens. It's not like they could walk out and find jobs that would pay even as well as Candless sweatshops." Angelo gave a shrug. "If I were one of them, Iso, as desperate to stay here and as powerless as they are, taking out a stoolie, even a woman, would seem like the only reasonable thing to do."

"And the Candless heirs would have killed two birds with one stone...oh, that's terrible. I mean—"

"I know what you mean." She just hadn't meant to be crass with her analogy to killing birds. "Someone *was* killed, Iso."

"Gina." She agreed. "Then, in your scenario, the INS investigation was stalled a little longer without Gina, giving Conrad the time to clean up any trace of illegal labor at Candless Industries. Everything was settled."

"Except that the shooters weren't really interested in killing an innocent baby who they had no clue existed. And no one counted on you saving him."

"Angelo, this is all just a lot of speculation! I mean, dear God, how can this have happened this way? Why wouldn't they have made absolutely certain that Seth was murdered along with his mother? He is really their problem, not Gina."

"We're only accounting for what did happen, Iso. There was Seth, there was ironclad confirmation of his paternity, there was the offer from Candless to Gina through St. John. The INS knew about it and tried to bring her into their investigation of abuses by Candless Industries. Then Gina Sellers is gunned down in broad daylight, in a neighborhood she had no business being in, by shooters who just happen to be illegal aliens... I don't know. Why would you worry that a five-month-old baby would survive a drive-by shooting? What else is there to conclude from the facts?"

Isobel shook her head. There seemed no other way to construe the events, the timing. "How are we ever going to prove any of this? Do the police have anything yet? They haven't connected the gunmen with Candless Industries' importing of illegal aliens, have they?"

"They have their suspicions, finally, but tying the two together doesn't necessarily do anything for their murder case. They have your account, but the other bystanders have told so many stories, there's no hope of sorting out the truth. They have the guns, the burn marks on the shooters' hands, the ballistics—all the physical evidence. But the perps aren't talking, and they've got *nada* from the woman whose house Gina had just departed before the murder. The woman's story has been that Gina must have come there by mistake, that she turned her away, and that's all there was to it. She hasn't deviated from her story once.''

''What was the woman's name?''

''Pilar Sanchez.''

Seth began to fuss. Isobel picked him up again, crooning comfort and love, then moved aside her clothes to nurse him. ''And the police have not tied Pilar to the gunmen?''

''Not with any certainty. She has her green card and she's been here for several years. No one has established a solid link to the shooters, and they've tried. She doesn't have a phone, so there are no telephone company logs to show whether a call was ever made to Gina from Pilar.''

Isobel gave an exasperated sigh. ''Why would they risk luring Gina to the barrio anyway? Why not just kill her where she lived, or where she shopped? Wouldn't they have stood a better chance of getting away with it off their own turf?''

''Not necessarily. They have the silence of the neighborhood. The eyewitness accounts are a jumble of lies. They're protecting their own. The us-against-them mentality is thick, Iso. It's what's destroying this country, this city. If I hadn't intervened, these guys would almost certainly have gotten away clean—even having to back up and get rid of Seth.''

"But if they weren't being exploited in the first place, this never would have—"

"I know. It's a hopeless cycle. The barrios, the ghettos." Angelo grimaced. "Pascal is probably right. Retribution and vengeance isn't going to cut it. Only love will finally make a difference."

Isobel laughed out loud at his sourpuss expression. An Avenging Angel of the Lord could hardly tolerate the pantywaist implications of love being the only answer in a world gone mad.

He looked at her longingly, then looked down, and Isobel knew in that telling instant that it was his love for her that made a dent in his fierce and fearsome sensibilities, that made him see how Pascal could be right.

She felt the battle going on inside his soul—the avenger and the angel now confronted with an even higher truth—and she sought a way to ease the path back to more familiar turf.

"What if we talked to Pilar?" she asked. "Maybe she didn't know she was setting Gina up to be murdered. If she has children of her own, even if she doesn't, I think she might talk to me. She probably didn't see me pick Seth up after Gina was murdered, but she must have seen the news reports and photographs. If we go to her and tell her we suspect someone else was behind the murder, maybe she would tell us what happened."

Angelo stared at her.

She flushed. "Am I being hopelessly naive again, or what? I think we could get Candless to let you take me to see Father Sifuentes, and Pilar lives very near there. It is a good idea, isn't it?"

Angelo gave a grudging half-smile. "No, Iso. For a mortal brain stem, my love, it is a brilliant idea."

ANGELO DEPARTED to prepare for his bodyguard position, leaving her under the watchful care of half a dozen Guardian Angels; Isobel took Seth to see Helena in the kitchen. He had begun this morning fretting and drooling with his first teething pains. She'd given the housekeeper a couple of teething rings to chill in the refrigerator.

Helena was nowhere to be found. Isobel retrieved one of the rings from the ice compartment, poured herself a lemonade and sat down at the glass-top table where she had confronted Harry last night.

Seth had begun to gum the teething ring in earnest, when Patrice Candless, dabbing her eyes with a handkerchief, darted into the kitchen. She caught sight of Isobel with Seth and stopped short, her hand on the refrigerator door.

"Is something wrong, Mrs. Candless?"

The woman tossed her head and sniffed. "Not that it's any concern of yours." She pulled open the refrigerator, took out the glass pitcher of lemonade and poured her own glass. Isobel had never seen her near the kitchen. "But yes. Bruce has sent for his things. I've set Helena to packing." She gulped. Fresh tears sprang to her eyes. "He has a condo in the city, of course. Has had for years. But he came here weekends, and of late, he's been staying more often."

Isobel murmured her sympathy. "This is not a good time, I know. I'm sorry."

"You know." Patrice dumped ice cubes into her glass and sat down to tame her agitation, her tone implying Isobel knew less than nothing about the subject. "I understand my husband has hired a body-guard for you."

Isobel cleared her throat. "For Seth." But she saw it would have been kinder not to draw attention to the distinction. The import was clear enough. Candless had hired a bodyguard to protect his new son from the rest of his own family.

"It's absurd," Patrice railed. Her blond hair was perfectly styled in a French roll, her makeup flawless even now, but there was such a fragile and hard-bitten aspect to her gestures and words that she seemed more claws than class, more defeated than daunting. "I know my children. They all have faults, certainly. I'm not blind to any of their faults. But murder?"

Isobel knew in her heart the resentment Patrice could only express in this sideways manner. She got up to gather a few paper towels to sop up Seth's fierce drooling, then traded sides of the cold teething between his sore gums. There wasn't anything as simple as a teething ring that she could say or do to ease Patrice's pain, especially since she believed one of Patrice's children, or all of them, *had* conspired to murder Gina Sellers. "I'm sure you'll miss Bruce. He seems very caring. Very loyal to you."

Patrice wrapped both her hands about her glass of lemonade and sighed. "He hasn't always been that way. Bruce has been angry at me most of his life."

"Why?"

"He wanted me to leave Ian. He couldn't abide the way we were treated, any of us. He never cared about himself. Nothing Ian could say or do ever really fazed him. He's a force to be reckoned with and always has been. Bruce was—is—the most stalwart soul I have ever known, child or man. But he hated what went on between Ian and me, and if he'd had his way, I'd have left this marriage before Kelsey was ever born. Or Harrison, for that matter.''

"He felt as if he had to protect you from his father?"

"I suppose he did." The older woman's chin trembled. "Considering all that's happened, he might as well have tilted at windmills."

"He must love you very much to have tried."

"But he never understood what his father went through, how he'd dragged himself up from the other side of the tracks in some backwater little Oklahoma town to where he is today."

"Perhaps not, but he is your son. From what you said, he understood clearly how much you were hurting."

Patrice would not be sidetracked. Some part of her insisted on defending Ian Candless even now, even after the worst of betrayals. "*I* understood him. I truly did. I do even now. Ian was under tremendous pressure, self-imposed and otherwise. He wanted his children to have what he never did. Once that happened, though, he half resented them for having everything he had fought so hard to provide."

Isobel more clearly understood Bruce's viewpoint than his mother's. Nothing in the world was worth having at the cost of making your children feel guilty for what you had given them. She despised the guilt.

But always at the back of her mind was a facet of Patrice's understanding, Isobel's own awareness that Ian Candless was victim, too. A victim who, even if he understood the suffering he caused in turn, even if in some perverse way he enjoyed it, didn't know how else to behave. How else to be.

But despite her defense of her husband against the ill opinion of his son Bruce, Patrice's pale blue eyes filled again.

Isobel got up to let Patrice compose herself and to get a fresh teething ring from the ice compartment, then settled back into her chair with Seth gnawing at the icy relief it provided. "Did Bruce ever convince you to consider leaving your husband?"

"No. I couldn't do that." She took a sip of her lemonade. Her hands, age-spotted and beginning to gnarl at her knuckles, shook. Her tears had abated, but she hadn't regained much of her composure. "Years ago I bought myself a little pearl-handled gun, though. I learned to use it. I meant to kill him. So many times."

Her voice had dropped to little more than a whisper. "I should have killed him. I should have done it. I should have taken the gun and put us all out of our misery. Lord knows I had provocation enough a dozen times. A hundred. But what he's done to this family now is despicable. It's beyond bad taste. He pulled himself up by the bootstraps with his wretched excess, and now he's rubbing all our noses in it. He's slime. He's—"

"Mrs. Candless—"

"Don't." She looked at Isobel now as if she couldn't believe she had said such things to the nanny of her husband's illegitimate son. "Don't offer me your platitudes or your warnings, Ms. Avedon." She looked for the first time at Seth with a terrible resentment. "My life is in a shambles, my family is destroyed, and my husband is responsible for all of it.''

Isobel understood. Nothing she could say would change the ill effects of Ian Candless's subtle and not-so-subtle abuses. "Did Bruce tell you why he's chosen to leave now? Does it have to do with Seth being here?"

"Less than you might imagine." Patrice swallowed hard. "Bruce and I have...reconciled, I guess one would say, in the last year. He's been a pillar of support. Very solicitous. Fiercely loyal to me. It's almost as if he knew, you know?" She swallowed again and dabbed at her eyes. "As if he somehow knew that the worst blow yet was coming to me. He has been the son I always dreamed he would be, but now he is leaving for good, and as far as I am concerned, that's on Ian's head as well."

She rambled on, almost as if Isobel were not there, for several more seconds, but Isobel didn't hear anymore after Patrice's pitiable speculation.

It's almost as if he knew.

SETH NAPPED most of the afternoon. Waiting for Angelo to return, Isobel paced the floor of the playroom, trying to decide what it was that Patrice suspected Bruce knew.

It wasn't outside the realm of possibility that Emory St. John was not the only member of the Candless clan who knew Gina was pregnant. Gina herself was well known to Bruce, since he was always the one to ferry her to her assignations with his father. Had they developed some kind of bond, a friendship? Wasn't it likely that Bruce knew of the baby even before his sister's husband became involved with leasing her condo?

But Gina had told St. John the baby was not Candless's. Would she have told Bruce just the opposite?

The only possibility that made sense of Bruce's emotional reconciliation with his mother was that Gina had confessed to him that her baby was the child of Ian Candless. Bruce must have feared that the whole thing would come out, and that when it did, his mother would be devastated.

The kindness he showed toward his mother was the only thing he knew to do. And if he had known all those months, then it was not likely he would have been involved in any conspiracy to murder Gina. He was a savvy, respected, wealthy businessman in his own right, and if he'd seen a way to bribe Gina, he would surely have done it before Seth was ever born. It seemed he'd have done anything to spare Patrice—anything short of murder—including keeping the secret from his brothers and sister.

Which ruled out only one of them. But Isobel was somehow certain that was what Bruce knew. Her heart went out to Patrice. She was not an unwitting woman. She knew of her husband's infidelities. Her humiliation could only have thrived, knowing what her son had tried to do to shield her from the worst of it.

And if Isobel had to guess, she would guess that Patrice knew, deep down in her heart where she kept secrets even from herself, that Bruce *had* known all along that Seth would destroy his mother's already fragile house of cards.

Angelo arrived at four o'clock, driving the BMW they had used before. He had spent two hours going over the territory encompassed by the Candless compound in the company of the security chief. By the time Isobel could share her thoughts with him, they were in the BMW headed to the barrio neighborhood where Pilar Sanchez lived and Gina Sellers had been murdered.

While he was away, Angelo had called Ian Candless, impersonating Father Ramon Sifuentes, asking to visit Isobel and Seth. Candless had suggested instead that they visit him, in the company of her bodyguard. The priest's arrival at the estate, he said, would cause too much speculation by the rabid journalists camped out near the entrance to the family compound.

When Isobel finally saw the press encampment through the dark-tinted glass of the BMW, she shrank low in her seat. She knew they could not see or photograph her or the baby in his infant seat. Still, the low-keyed frenzy made her shudder.

When they had cleared the gauntlet of cameras, she straightened. "I can't believe Candless let us take Seth off the estate. Did you hypnotize him or what?"

Angelo gave her a sidelong glance. "You are always accusing me of these nefarious deeds, Iso. What have I done to make you so skeptical?"

"Oh, please. You have done everything but put them all into a coma and invite the INS in to ransack the estate."

"Well, Candless believes it was his idea for the baby to have an outing."

"Which is so out of character for him as to make me accuse you yet again."

"Whatever it takes, Iso." He flashed her a grin.

"Finish telling me what happened with Patrice Candless."

Isobel filled him in on her accidental meeting and conversation with Patrice, leaving out nothing, concluding with her speculation that it was almost as if Bruce had known another blow was coming.

"Do you think she's still considering using her pearl-handled gun?"

"I don't know, Angelo. She's had enough of the grief and humiliation. More than enough. Thirty years or more."

Isobel looked carefully at Angelo, at the fully human male he was now. The five-o'clock shadow, the tiny hairs on his knuckles, the way his little finger creased on the steering wheel. His presence as an angel in the guise of a human being was always more ethereal, less real, somehow.

Fully human, his body consumed air, took up space, radiated heat. She couldn't breathe without taking in the air they shared, or fail to feel the warmth or smell the clean, utterly masculine scent he generated.

"How is it that you can read my mind all the time, and not know what is in everyone else's?"

He gave her a disbelieving look. "Think of the chaos, Iso, if I heard everyone's thoughts."

"I'm serious, Angelo!" She glanced into the back seat. Seth was dozing lightly, lulled by the motion and low vibrations of the BMW engine.

He swallowed, on some disappointment she thought. Disappointment in her.

"What?" she demanded, half afraid to hear how she had let him down.

"The bond we share, Isobel Avedon, is uncommon."

Now she swallowed hard. It was the done thing, among angels, to have such intimate access to the thoughts of one another. And it was the done thing for Guardian Angels and Avenging Angels to influence the thoughts of their charges in favor of better choices—even to plant in their mortal heads thoughts that would not otherwise have occurred to them, just as Angelo had influenced Candless to suggest the baby should go on this outing with them.

But Isobel didn't know how it was supposed to work between Angelo and her…hadn't known that it was the bond between them, and not any higher angelic powers of his, that gave him access to her thoughts.

"I don't know how it will come to be, Iso, but what is between us is not going away. Not in this or any other lifetime. We are meant to be together. It would mean a great deal to me if you could find it in your heart to put some faith in us."

Her turn, she thought raggedly, breathlessly, to swallow hard again. The same swaggering attitude that had galled her to no end in every moment up to this, galled her no more. She would be his, as he would be hers. She knew it. What finally swayed her opinion she could not have said, but Isobel Avedon finally believed.

THE CHEAP TRACT HOUSE where Pilar Sanchez lived, no more than fifty yards from where Gina Sellers had been shot to death, lay silent. Though dusk had fallen, there were no lights, no sounds coming from inside, not so much as a radio. But for Angelo's still extraordinary powers of observation, they would not have known Pilar was at home.

She was.

They walked up the sidewalk to the cracking cement stoop, Isobel toting Seth, and Angelo rang the doorbell.

The door opened a couple of inches. From the darkened interior, a small Hispanic woman looked out at Isobel, then prayed softly, calling upon the Mother of God. "You are the one to save the baby."

"Yes. My name is Isobel Avedon. This is my...my friend, Angelo. May we come inside a few moments and talk to you?"

She shook her head rapidly. "I have told the police everything I know—"

"Please," Angelo interrupted, slipping into a soft, sonorous plea in Spanish.

Isobel didn't know what he'd said. The exchange went on a few more seconds, then the woman opened the door and gestured them hurriedly inside.

She asked them to make themselves comfortable on an old orange plaid sofa, and took for herself a small, worn rocker covered in an inexpensive celery-colored velvet. Her gaze rested on Seth.

"It is a miracle that you saved this sweet baby." She crossed herself, offering a small prayer for the baby's mother.

"I think so too," Isobel responded warmly. "He is precious, isn't he?"

"*Si*. Precious." Pilar Sanchez began to wring her hands, glancing back and forth between Isobel and Angelo. "I had nothing to do with the mother's death. I—"

Again, Angelo soothed her fears, calling her by

name. "Don't worry at all, Pilar. We believe you knew nothing of what would happen. There are others who intended the baby's death, and his mother's. We think they used you. That they lied to you."

Pilar shook her head, denying even that much. "I know nothing of this."

Angelo took a newspaper clipping from his jacket pocket and handed it to Isobel to pass to the woman.

"Pilar," she began softly, "please look at this photograph. It was in all the newspapers several days ago. I'm there in front, with the baby. See? Can you tell us if you recognize anyone else?"

Pilar took the clipping, lifted the glasses that hung around her neck by a chain, and looked at the photo for several seconds, her gaze moving slowly, left to right, studying the faces of the Candless family with whom Isobel had posed her first night on the estate.

Still looking, she shook her head. "I'm sorry, I don't—" she broke off.

A hissing noise came from her lips, and Pilar Sanchez went starkly still.

Chapter Thirteen

"Who are these people?"

Isobel exchanged looks with Angelo. "They are the family of the baby's father, Ian Candless."

"No," Pilar insisted. "It is not possible."

"That someone in this photo wanted to kill this baby and his mother?" Angelo demanded gently. "One of them came to you, is that right? One of them asked you to do something, to get this baby's mother to come here?"

She clapped a bony hand over her mouth to stifle her cry.

Isobel reached out to cover the woman's other hand with her own. "Which one of them came to you, Pilar?"

Tears sprang to Pilar's eyes, splashing her glasses. She jerked them off and let them fall on their chain. Her head never stopped shaking back and forth, denying, Isobel thought, what she was seeing, that one of the baby's own family would arrange his mother's murder. His own murder, for that had been the intention.

"Can you at least tell us what happened?"

Pilar struggled to regain her equilibrium. She took

a tissue from the sleeve of her sweater and mopped her eyes. "I tell you, I had no notion that anyone would die."

"But one of these people asked you to get the baby's mother to come here, to your home?"

"Yes. I was told that the woman I should contact was an INS agent. I was told that she knew where to find my grandchildren and my great-grandchildren, who only managed to come to this country two years ago, and do not have green cards. I thought they would be deported and thrown into prison in Mexico. I was told that if I offered this woman other information, she would turn a blind eye to my...to my family."

"What other information?" Angelo asked.

"I didn't know. This...I was told the information would be delivered to me, and that I could hand it over to the INS woman. That I shouldn't worry. But when the time came, I had nothing. I sent her away. What else could I do?" She gave a keening cry, her hands tightly clasped between her knees. "What else could I do?" She clamped her teeth together, jutting her chin resentfully, as angry now as she was scared. "What kind of INS agent comes to your door with a baby in her arms, can you tell me that, *señor*?"

Angelo drew a deep breath. "No kind of agent I know, Pilar, comes to your door with a baby in her arms."

"Then this was all a lie?" she demanded.

"You were tricked," Isobel answered. "Are your grandchildren all right? Have you heard from them?"

"Yes. But Paco, who is in your jails for driving the car where the shooting came from." Her face pinched tightly. "They tricked him, too. Tricked him good, but he would rather lose his life than break the silence and condemn his friends and family."

"Was there no way you could tell all of this to the police?" Isobel asked, her heart aching for the old Hispanic woman who had done well enough for herself and learned the language, only to have her grandchildren threatened and tricked and jailed.

"For what? Paco would say I am old and loco. And if they believed me, I would go to jail as well. I am the one who asked the baby's mother to come here," she finally admitted. "I am the one."

"Pilar," Angelo coaxed gently, "we may be able to help you, but our hands are tied unless you tell us which one of these people came to you and tricked you into this terrible scheme."

The old woman straightened, and though the scrawny wattle beneath her chin quivered, she pointed to Kelsey Candless St. John. "This one. She is with child, no?"

FOR THE SAKE of appearances, they visited Father Ramon Sifuentes in the small study of the battered church where Isobel had sought safety. When they left, the cleric was under the impression that they had spent a couple of hours, rather than only a few minutes, visiting together.

The drive back to the Candless compound stretched interminably. The Los Angeles traffic could not have been worse. Isobel changed Seth and nursed him to sleep before she could even begin to think about the implications of what Pilar Sanchez had told them.

Angelo had the radio tuned to a music station that

was playing an Argentine prelude on the classical guitar. He drummed his fingers on the steering wheel, caught up between the music and the driving. Even fully human, he could focus on half a dozen things at once.

She lifted the sleeping baby to her shoulder and patted his back. "What are you thinking?"

He waited until the end of the prelude. He knew the piece was nearly done, and he needed a moment to construct a lie. His head was full of images now, like slivers of half-remembered nightmares. Ever since the moment when Pilar Sanchez had pointed an accusing finger at Kelsey St. John, he'd known the rot had seeped farther and deeper into the Candless family than he had imagined. From Ian to his sons to his daughter.

Patrice Candless would have done the world a huge favor if she had taken her little pearl-handled gun and shot the son of a bitch before he could poison all of his children.

She hadn't.

The images in his head, though, had only to do with Iso. He saw her as if lit by a strobe in the dark of a movie house, turning her head, jerk by tiny jerk, until she saw a thing that made her cry out, saw the thing and looked to Angelo. She knew he couldn't save her. He saw her cry out again, screaming out how she loved him, how she would love him unto eternity, how she must do the thing that would end her life, how she turned, how, degree by degree, she exposed her back to protect the baby, how she slumped like a rag doll collapsing to the floor...

How the blood seeped out the hole where the bullet tore into her body.

The images blurred in his mind. He couldn't see where or when, couldn't see how the fractured images began. All he knew was that he was witnessing Isobel's death. And so when she asked what it was he was thinking about, he had to lie.

He lowered the volume on the radio and looked at her. "I miss this, Iso. I miss music. Concerts. You know there was such an incredible explosion of musical genius after the Renaissance. After we...after we died. The instruments, the composers."

She smiled, and he knew he had succeeded in his lie. He couldn't have carried a tune in a basket himself, but Angelo de Medici in any age was a sucker for a passionate piece of music. And so she believed him, didn't see that his human heart was on the verge of exploding in his fear that the vision reflected the future. That it would come true.

"I meant about Pilar, silly. About Kelsey."

"I know." He embellished on the lie. "But there are so many things I want to do with you. Places I want to take you. You haven't really lived until you've heard Beethoven's Fifth played under the stars in the Vail valley."

"Maybe we can even go there and live."

He darted a look at her. He couldn't breathe.

"How's that for faith in us, de Medici?"

Inside himself he died a thousand mortal deaths. She had come to believe, to accept that what he said was true, to have faith in his promises that he would not let her die, that what was between them would never end in this or any lifetime, that they would be together forever, even when this was done. And now this eerie sensation, this foreboding he couldn't fathom, a sudden bolt of alarm, like a lightning strike from a clear blue sky.

If the images were true, and not his half-human consciousness throwing irrational dread into the mix of emotions, Isobel had come to believe just in time to have her "ever after" stripped from her again.

He thought their bond only went one way, that he could know so easily what she was thinking, but she saw the sudden and alien fear in him. "Angelo… What is it? What's wrong?"

"I'm a little surprised." He made it sound as if, all things being equal, he should have known Kelsey was deeply involved, and that he was troubled by this apparent failure.

"Good old Kelsey is right there in the thick of things."

He could feel her eyes on him, feel her doubt that he was telling her the truth. He made an impenetrable vault of his mind, blocking her, making her remember that angels cannot lie.

What did it mean, that he was lying to her now, when angels could not lie, except in the interests of justice in the case of an Avenging Angel. What did it mean?

He returned to the subject of Kelsey's involvement. "I was trying to figure out if St. John knows this and was just feeding us a line of bull, or if it's even possible he doesn't know."

Against her instincts, he knew, Isobel accepted his lies, believing this was what was on his mind. "I don't think St. John knows. If I were Kelsey, I sure wouldn't tell him. Who else would?"

"No one, before the deed was done. But once Gina was dead, it would have eased their guilty hearts to make sure the attorney in the family knew exactly what had gone on.''

He turned onto the road leading to the guard house and waited until the gates had been opened. Driving through, he gestured acknowledgment to the guard, then drove the BMW to its assigned space in the Candless garages. The sun would sink into the watery horizon in another half hour.

He went around the car and helped Isobel out, reaching, like any fully human father might, for the diaper bag and discarded blanket on the back seat.

Flashing again on the specter of Isobel's death, he longed for mortal ignorance, for an ordinary life, for such oddly comforting drudgery as a human father knows. He didn't want to believe Isobel would die. He couldn't. But the images kept flying at him, and he took them for a warning. He had never in his five hundred years been more alert, more wary. Or more deeply afraid.

The front door was opened to them by the housekeeper, Helena, but otherwise they saw no one on their way to the nursery suite. Isobel placed Seth on his tummy in the crib and reached above him to wind up the music box in the mobile of clowns. Angelo put his arm around her. She rested her head on his shoulder, and they stood together over the slumbering baby for a long moment.

She turned to him then, circling his waist with her arms. ''I want this for us, Angelo. I want it so much.''

Struck again with the depth of her acceptance, that they would have this because he had promised her that they would, he held her tight. His throat tightened, and his groin, and he knew if he was ever, ever to keep his promise, it would be because he behaved now like the bodyguard he was supposed to be, and not a mortal male swamped with mortal desires, mortal longings.

Mortal ineptitudes.

He trembled in his body and breathed deeply, inhaling the essence of her one last time. The moment of ultimate truth was coming, he knew, coming fast now, and he would not be caught off guard, necking with Isobel as he had in that palace courtyard five hundred years ago, touching her, exciting them both to the point where he no longer smelled danger when sensing the threat was all that he was about.

He separated from her and guided her out into the light of the playroom. "I need to listen to the tapes, Iso."

She touched a finger to her lips and held it out to him, and he did the same. Their fingers met, and curled together, embracing in a clandestine, secret sort of kiss they had conjured together centuries before. Isobel took up a book of children's poetry and sat down on the sofa. Across from her, he took the easy chair where he usually listened to the audiotapes of each conversation that had gone on in the household that day.

He punched into the cell phone the set of seventeen numbers necessary to access the tapes by remote instructions, opted for the highest transmission speed, and then sat listening as tape after tape cued up. Halfway through, he began focusing with greater intensity, trebling his concentration. He watched Isobel look up from the book of children's poetry, so finely attuned to every nuance of his body language that she knew what he was hearing was what they had awaited so long.

"What is it?"

He held up a hand to her, indicating she should wait. At the end of the tape, he keyed in several more numbers, signaling the playback equipment to rewind. At the beginning of the conversation, he slowed the playback, put the cell phone down and caused it to act as a speakerphone.

"Here it is, Iso. Finally. The Feds have not heard it yet, but they will."

A voice stamp identified the recording. "St. John residence, study of Emory St. John, tape number 151."

There were a couple of moments when movement into and about the room could be heard, but no voices. Then a knock came at a door.

"Come in." St. John's voice.

"We have to talk. Now." Conrad's voice, followed by Kelsey's agreement.

"What do you want?"

"I want to know what you're doing about this mess, Sinjin. What the hell's going on? What is it with the old man and the nanny?"

"What am *I* doing? I'm pedaling as fast as I bloody can trying to establish some damage control. What are *you* doing?"

"Look—" Conrad began.

"No, you look," Sinjin interrupted. "Your *father* now suspects that you, the three of you, maybe all of us, conspired to bribe Gina Sellers, rather than Gina Sellers ever trying to extort us. Your *father* is all over me about this illegal-alien business." He swore. "Even the freaking nanny knows you all had a motive for murder, so what do you think your father suspects?"

Conrad matched his brother-in-law for expletives. "If you had a clue, Sinjin, what it's like for the old man to be all over you, you'd know why the hell I started down this road."

"I warned you—"

"Oh yeah. You warned me. But I'm the one who had to cut labor costs. I had no other choice but to start importing cheap labor."

"No choice." Sinjin's voice oozed deep sarcasm.

"You arrogant ass! You think it isn't what goes on in the real world? You think every other clothing manufacturer out there isn't ass-deep in illegals? Think again. And while you're at it, think again about murder, Sinjin. I didn't do it, Kelsey didn't do it, Harrison hasn't got the *cojones* to take out a flea, and Bruce—"

"Oh, you're a fine one to talk *cojones*," Harrison interrupted angrily. "If you had the brains God gave a brick, you'd be dangerous."

"Stop it, both of you," Kelsey cried. "We can't be fighting among ourselves. Not now. What's done is done."

Isobel looked at Angelo. He nodded.

"This is it, isn't it?" she asked excitedly. "The Feds have Conrad on tape admitting to having imported illegal alien labor."

Angelo paused the playback with phone cues. "This is it, Iso. This is exactly what they want." He let hope seep into him, through every cell in his mortal body. He could get Isobel out of here now, out of danger, out of any scenario where the fragmented images of her foreshadowed death might become reality.

"Is there more?"

"Like a confession to the murder of Gina Sellers?" He grinned. The relief inside him was so thick, so overwhelming he couldn't help it. He *would* get her out of here now, and she wasn't going to die. "No. But very nearly. Listen to this."

He punched a couple of numbers on the cell phone and the tape picked up with Kelsey's angry interruption.

"Stop it, both of you. We can't be fighting among ourselves. Not now. What's done is done."

"What are you talking about, Kelsey?" St. John demanded. "'Not now.' What is that supposed to mean?"

"Nothing," she snapped. "Just—nothing. Let it go, will you? If just once you would stand up and be a man and do what had to be done, Sinjin," she hissed, "then—oh, what the hell. It doesn't matter. Some of us do what has to be done, and some of us sit around wringing our hands about it. I'm warning you, if you don't get my father off our cases and find a way to get rid of that bastard brat and his nanny, I will leave you. I swear I will."

"Holy mother, you did it, didn't you?"

"Take a chill, Sinjin," Harrison spat. "You don't know what you're talking about."

"You set Gina Sellers up to be murdered didn't you?" St. John's strangled voice swore vilely, plainly shocked. "Didn't you?"

"Let go of me!" Kelsey cried out.

"Get your hands off my sister, Sinjin," Conrad

threatened, "or I swear I'll take you out where you stand."

"Get out of my house," Sinjin snarled. "All of you. Get out of my house."

"I'm leaving, Sinjin," Kelsey taunted. "But don't ever forget. This is not, and never has been, your house."

A door slammed, and all that was left was the sound of Emory St. John sinking into his chair.

Angelo turned off the phone. Isobel wrapped her arms about her waist. She looked pale to him, suddenly more fragile than he knew her to be. "Should you call them, the INS," she asked, "and let them know what's on this tape?"

"They will have heard it by morning, Iso." He wanted to make her feel better, to see the end in sight beyond the ugliness on that tape. "We'll be out of here in less than twenty-four hours. Twelve, maybe."

"I'm not going without Seth."

"We've got enough here to make a decent case for removing him from this estate."

"But that will take longer, won't it?"

He looked at her. "If we do it legally, yes."

She lowered her gaze from his and swallowed. "I want it done right, Angelo. It has to be done right so that I can have him for all time. So we can have him."

"Then we'll stay until it's done legally." He half expected the quivering sensation, the same foreboding, the images of her death to assault him, but none of that happened.

She shivered hard, but straightened, nodding her agreement. "Would you…would you mind terribly staying the night with me, in my bed with me?"

Touched deeply in his soul, Angelo nodded. But in his heart of hearts he feared Isobel was hedging her bets against the possibility that if he didn't lie with her this night, he never would again.

HE MADE LOVE TO HER for hours on end, hours more precious to her than all the treasures laid up in heaven or on earth. But when she fell asleep, the nightmares began.

Her mind replayed over and over the scene in the palace courtyard, and every time—every time—the face of Angelo's brother mocked her, his head thrown back filling the jasmine-scented night air with his maniacal laughter.

She struggled up from the depths of her anguished dream repeatedly. Angelo held her close, soothed her, stroked her forehead with his lips, but whenever she fell asleep again, the same dream would begin anew.

The treachery, the betrayal of his brother, his own flesh and blood haunted her. What was it? Why? Why this night?

But then, near dawn—she knew the time because with her maternal ear she heard Seth's first half-waking, half-sleeping morning cries—the dream changed, and it was Seth who consumed her dreams…and not Seth. He looked as he always looked, so sweet, so loving, so full of himself—like Angelo in that way, with his attitude full-blown. The dream made no sense, of course. She would call out to Seth, and though he was not of an age to respond, she knew he should.

In her dream, she knew he should. But maybe she

was mistaken. Maybe he was the wrong baby, or she was the wrong mother or the wrong father...

And then he began to fade from her sight, as if he were on some kind of evil magic carpet transporting him away from her. She called out to him and he began to cry. He reached for her, but she couldn't reach him no matter what she did, how fast she ran.

This time, Angelo woke her. She was crying. Tears ran down her cheeks. She darted from the bed to go check on the baby, and found him owl-eyed, just waking, waiting for her, breaking into an all-over smile for her. She dashed the tears from her cheeks and changed his diaper and lifted him up to take him back to bed with her.

Feeding the babe, she described the dreams to Angelo. A sense of what her dreams portended came to her as she talked. He listened carefully. Respectfully. He knew, as all angels know, that mortal dreams are a reflection of understanding beyond the pale of normal human awareness. "What do you think they mean, Iso?"

She looked at him, searching his eyes. "I think there is more that we don't know of Gina's murder, Angelo. Your brother betrayed you. I think that's the important part, that there must be betrayals here that we haven't uncovered."

He agreed with her interpretation, though neither of them could guess in what way there were other betrayals in play around the murder of Gina Sellers. "What about Seth? The part about you being the wrong mother, or the wrong father?"

Isobel shook her head. "Angelo, I think the dream meant that Ian Candless is not Seth's father."

Angelo prayed to God she was right, and feared to the depths of his soul that she was wrong.

THE SAN JOSE INSTITUTE of Reproductive Technologies was housed on the tenth, eleventh and twelfth floors of a typical office building in the city. The reception area was fashionably done in mauve, ivory and teal blue, and the artwork didn't come from any half-baked gallery. Steeped in money, the institute's reputation for quality control, accuracy and the highest rate of success in any reproductive endeavor made it a world-class facility.

Angelo reassured Isobel as they entered the building and took the elevator to the tenth floor. "The Institute personnel will be cooperative, Iso. Their reputation is at stake in high-profile cases like this."

They had left the estate to answer a request to meet with the district attorney's investigators. Candless had been told, in a phone call made by Angelo in the guise of the D.A., that it was essential to verify Seth's identity by a match to the HLA markers performed with the paternity testing.

The excuse had worked well enough. Candless didn't like it, but there could be no reason to refuse to have his infant son positively identified. Now, having only Isobel's gut feeling to go on, they were about to take on this world-class facility and its employees, questioning them as to the integrity of the paternity report on Ian James Candless.

They had discussed various ruses, beginning with some other function of the lab than paternity testing. *In vitro* fertilization records were the obvious choice. But the ruse would be time-consuming and ultimately pointless—the lab personnel would ultimately know, or at least have strong reason to suspect, that the Candless files had been the original target of the investigation.

They would, instead, count on the intimidation factor of Candless himself having called into question the results.

The receptionist glanced up, saw Isobel holding Seth and assumed they were former clients whose name she couldn't quite place. Isobel took the initiative to get over her butterflies.

"Thank you, but we are not former patients. My name is Isobel Avedon—"

"I knew I'd seen you before!" the receptionist cried. "You're the woman who they thought kidnapped the Candless baby. And this must be him!"

Angelo nodded. "Yes. And I am Angelo de Medici, representing Ian Candless. We're here to examine the test results that concluded Mr. Candless was in fact the baby's father."

"Is there some problem?"

Angelo let his expression speak for itself. "I'd like to see the lab director."

"Oh." The slight, sandy-blond woman laughed nervously. "I'm afraid our director, Dr. Gilbraithe, is out this week, and that is who—"

"We don't need to see Dr. Gilbraithe today," Angelo interrupted, oozing Latin charm. "If you'd like, introduce us to whoever is in charge at the moment."

"If you'll just take a seat," the receptionist stalled, "I'll see who I can find."

Angelo leaned in instead, resting one forearm on the counter. "Karen Jelniker. Page her for us, now." He smiled. His attentive gaze, as if he were looking at the only other human being left on earth, made a woman go buttery inside. Isobel knew from long experience. "Please," he added.

The receptionist sank into her chair and paged Karen Jelniker. Her internal line rang almost immediately. She grabbed it up and told Jelniker that there were representatives of a former client to see her.

Angelo thanked the receptionist. Karen Jelniker appeared. Introductions were made. Isobel felt her stomach tighten. Unlike Angelo, she had no experience at fishing expeditions.

"What a sweet baby! How old is he?"

"Five months."

Jelniker led them to her office. Seated behind the desk, she asked, "How may I help you?"

Angelo waited for Isobel to select her chair, then took the other one opposite the supervisor's desk. "I'll come straight to the point, Ms. Jelniker. Ian Candless believes the results you reported as to his paternity of this child are in error."

"Well, you are absolutely welcome to examine the test results. I'll just call in—"

She was interrupted by a phone call. She answered, listened a moment, then put the caller on hold. "I'm afraid I have to take this call, but let me direct you to the technologist who performed the testing. It was Cassidy Roper. You'll find her down the hall, the third door on your left. I'll let her know you're coming."

The technologist was just hanging up her phone when Isobel and Angelo arrived at her door. The space was cramped. She greeted them coolly and suggested a conference room. She smiled. "I'm afraid the slave labor around here doesn't rate corner offices."

Isobel felt there was something very off about the technologist's tone of voice, or what she said, or how she was acting. She exchanged glances with Angelo as Cassidy Roper ushered them into a small conference room. "If you'll wait here, I'll get the records you want to see."

Angelo stopped her. "We may just need to talk to you for a moment, Ms. Roper. We are not qualified to interpret your tests in any case."

She gave a bright nod. "Is this the baby in question?"

Angelo nodded, but his lack of a smile in return was enough to frost the air. "If we took a sample of the baby's blood today, say, would they match the results you got before?"

"Of course. We wouldn't have the reputation we do if we couldn't guarantee the integrity and reproducibility of our results."

"Would you be willing to do that for us? Take the baby's blood and retest?"

She seemed inexplicably to relax, becoming somehow more genuine and less obsequious.

Angelo thanked her. Isobel didn't have a clue what he was up to. They hadn't talked about testing Seth again, or forcing the lab to duplicate its work. She knew he had something in mind, though.

"Would you retest the father's blood as well?"

The technologist agreed. "Certainly. Just have Mr. Candless come in and give us another sample—"

"That won't be necessary."

She looked at Angelo in surprise. "I'm sorry, but it is necessary if you want—"

"You don't understand, Ms. Roper. You see, I am the father, and no one has yet tested my blood."

Chapter Fourteen

Stunned by Angelo's strategy and the bald-faced lie, Isobel almost laughed out loud. It didn't matter who the baby's father was, only that they knew, or that she felt, that Candless was not.

The technologist blanched. "That's impossible."

"Why?"

"Because—"

"Because why, Ms. Roper? Because you falsified the report? Because you thought no one knew who the baby's father was? How did you do it?"

Flushing angrily, the tech scraped a hand through her hair. She started several times to deny Angelo's allegation, but his silence, his penetrating, accusing stare forbade her instinctive impulse to lie.

Her head bobbed nervously. She bit her lip and then defiantly shook her head. "All right. Fine. I falsified the report. Is that what you want me to say?"

"We want the truth, Ms. Roper."

Isobel began to shake. The relief inside her came in a torrent. She wouldn't have to fight Candless for Seth, wouldn't have to go up against all that money and the legal wrangling it could buy. She lowered her head and kissed the top of Seth's, holding him tighter than she should have, then looked at the technologist. "Why?"

"Why? Because I needed the money. Because I was offered fifty thousand dollars. Trust me," she said, her lips shaping into a sneer, "that family could afford it. And the baby got a silver spoon in his mouth. Who was hurt?"

"His mother was murdered because of it," Angelo answered.

"That's not my fault. They have so damned much money they can wipe somebody out and get away with it. How is that my fault?"

Angelo shook his head. There were still so many mortals who could justify any act or any lie at all. "Tell me how you did it."

She gave a scoffing sound. "It isn't hard. I performed the tests on the baby's and the mother's blood. Then I determined which cell markers were needed to match the baby's and confirm paternity. Then I added those markers to the test sample and reported them as belonging to Mr. Candless—which made his paternity a ninety-nine-point-nine percent certainty."

ANGELO FELT in his element now. He knew what had happened, knew what had to be done. This was the moment he looked forward to as no other, the moment when he confronted the mortals who had chosen in whatever manner suited them to flout the laws of God and man.

He had relished hundreds, thousands of such moments over the half millennium he had served in the capacity of an Avenging Angel of the Lord. Each and every time he had thought, *now*. With *this* one he could feel as if he had done enough, fought enough on the side of righteousness, brought enough justice into the world, that he could let go of his single unwitting failure.

He had died, *Isobel* had died, because of his mortal ineptitude. Because he was so enamored he never sensed the treachery coming. So if he could just right one more wrong, maybe he would have made up for that.

It was never enough. Never. This time, it would be. This time, Isobel lived and would live on, and justice would be done, and he could put an end to his calling as an Avenging Angel. He could do something else for the rest of eternity, having done not only what he had to do, but what had to be done in the name of justice for five hundred years.

This time spelled the end, and the relief inside him was exactly as human as the relief Isobel knew when she realized Ian Candless had no claim to the babe whom she loved more than she loved her place in heaven.

Angelo took out his cell phone on the way back to the Candless estate, called the INS, confirmed that they had heard the tapes that contained the incriminating words of the Candless heirs.

The INS offered to go in and make the arrests, absolving Isobel of any obligation to return to the estate. Angelo refused. There was the matter of the falsified identification of the baby. The technologist had confessed, certainly, but she didn't know who it was who had bribed and then paid her off after she turned out the report confirming Candless's paternity. Angelo intended to find out, and then the INS could storm the fortress to its heart's content.

Watching Angelo maneuver the BMW through the early afternoon traffic, Isobel felt her heart swell with happiness and pride. Seth would be hers forever after. Theirs. She knew it with a certainty that went beyond reason, just as she knew they would have their lifetime together.

And in the meanwhile, in the next few hours, she would have the privilege of watching Angelo accomplish the ends of justice in a manner befitting his role as an Avenging Angel. His attitude, which had galled her to no end, brought her nothing now save a fierce pride in who he was, and what he did in the service of mankind.

When the fear of returning to the clutches of Ian Candless raised its ugly head in her soul, Isobel refused to experience it. Angelo was more than his or any other mortal's match. She and Seth would be safe. And in a little while, both of them would be safe in Angelo's arms, far away from here in the beautiful Vail valley in Colorado.

FROM OUT OF NOWHERE, Angelo produced a transcript of the conversation between Sinjin, Kelley, Conrad and Harrison, and when they entered Candless's study in the main house, he tossed it on the man's desk.

Candless was unamused at the interruption and the impudence of a bodyguard he had employed. He rose from his cherrywood desk, his fingers planted, as if for a runner's sprint, on its surface. "What is the meaning of this?"

Isobel's heart thundered. Angelo merely narrowed his eyes. "I suggest you read it."

What Angelo, the Avenging Angel of the Lord

suggested, Ian Candless seemed unable to oppose. He sank back into his chair and took up the transcript.

An accomplished man, undoubtedly used to reading quickly to get to the bottom line, Candless skimmed, paled, then read more closely from beginning to end. When he had finished, he looked up. His handsome features seemed flat and uninterested, but his color was bad.

"Is this some kind of joke?"

"This, sir," Angelo retorted, "is no joke."

"Who are you?" he demanded. "Who the hell do you think you are? And you, missy, you with the *ovarios*—"

"Don't," Angelo warned him. "Don't even think it. Ms. Avedon is not a nanny, nor am I a bodyguard in your employ. We are undercover agents, Candless, and your family is in deep-ass trouble. I suggest you call them together now. With that transcript, you have only scratched the surface of a very ugly problem."

And again, what Angelo had suggested, Candless set into motion.

IT TOOK SEVERAL HOURS for everyone to gather at the estate. Bruce would not have come at all if Patrice, scared out of her mind by the fury in her husband's eyes, had not gotten on the line to beg him to come.

He was probably the only one, Isobel thought, who had any idea of the danger the summons home portended. The rest were simply too self-involved and put out with the peremptory demand even to question it. But then, all of them depended in the most basic way on Ian Candless for their lives and livelihoods.

None of them could afford to refuse. It seemed to Isobel, who listened with Angelo as Candless made each call to be certain no other communications were given, that his adult children and son-in-law were not unaccustomed to command performances at the drop of a hat.

By the time the family had all gathered, in Candless's study, sealed off from the eyes and ears of the servants, the sun prepared to set over the Pacific.

The view from this west-facing room was nothing less than spectacular. A peculiar excitement buzzed inside Isobel for the metaphor that came to her mind. When the sun had set on this day, this would be all over. Candless would know Seth was not his son. Angelo and Seth would be hers, the heinous murder of Gina Sellers would be avenged.

There were places enough for everyone to sit. Only Harrison stood, looking out the floor-to-ceiling window.

Patrice sat alone, huddled in on herself, wearing a sweater, her hands buried beneath it. Having flatly refused her request that he sit next to her on the elegant antique settee, Bruce sat on a stool at the wet bar. Isobel and Angelo stood behind and to the right of Candless.

Kelsey, Sinjin and Conrad took the club chairs fanning out from the desk.

"Okay," Bruce said, exquisitely bored by the gathering. "What's going on?"

Candless looked at his eldest son, then seemed to dismiss him. He rose behind his desk and picked up the transcript and began to read.

St. John residence, study of Emory St. John, tape number 151. A knock.

Sinjin. "Come in."

Conrad. "We have to talk. Now."

Kelsey. "Mmm."

Sinjin. "What do you want?"

Conrad. "I want to know what you're doing about this mess, Sinjin. What the hell's going on? What is it with the old man and the nanny?"

Sinjin. "What am I doing? I'm pedaling as fast as I bloody can trying to establish some damage control. What are you doing?"

Conrad. "Look—"

Sinjin. "No, you look. Your father now suspects that you, the three of you, maybe all of us, conspired to bribe Gina Sellers, rather than Gina Sellers ever trying to extort us. Your father is all over me about this illegal alien business. Even the freaking nanny knows you all had a motive for murder, so what do you think your father suspects?"

Candless looked up from his reading. The room was utterly silent. "Need I go on?"

Hatred glittered in Kelsey's eyes. "You bastard! You creepy, insane, paranoid old bastard! Is this whole damned estate bugged for your edification?"

Bruce's smile chilled the room. "Oh, this is rich."

"Shut up, you ass!" Kelsey spat. "You with your fancy plans and your promises. What good are you? What the hell did you ever do for any of us? Nothing. Nothing!" she cried. "You left us all here with him—"

"You wouldn't have gone anywhere there wasn't freaking money, Kelsey," he retorted.

"Silence." Candless's features hardened. He had never looked more his age, more absolutely betrayed. "I guess I may assume this transcript is an accurate reflection of the truth." He quelled Conrad's protest with a single vilifying look. "Whose brilliant idea was it to set up poor, ignorant, illegal immigrants to murder Gina Sellers?"

"That would be me, Dad," Harrison said, stepping forward, claiming his deed and, Isobel thought, his freedom from the stifling paranoia his father had inflicted on him. "Glad to see that, before you knew it was me at least, you recognized an exquisite *dénouement* to your little affair."

"Whatever possessed you?" Candless demanded, his pulse thumping at every visible vein in his neck and head.

"Opportunity. The ultimate gamble. There are more photo ops out there than you can imagine, Dad. For instance, Conrad here, cutting the deal to bring illegals over the border. Then there was Kelsey, threatening an old woman with her family being deported while the old girl did Kels's nails. Next came you, on the yacht with Gina Sellers. And last, but certainly not least, the INS agents talking to good old Gina. It didn't take but a few of those photos to effectively demonstrate to a couple of Conrad's illegal laborers that their ass was grass if Gina Sellers lived."

Isobel clutched Angelo's hand. Across from her, Patrice sat clutching her stomach, so sickened with dismay at what she was hearing that she sat silently crying.

They had had it figured correctly without knowing which of the three Candless heirs had hatched the plan. Of course it would be timid, guilt-stricken Harrison, willing to do anything at all to return the shock of the unnatural and cruel favors his father had done him in his lifetime.

But it was Bruce who sat stunned, his jaw slackened. "You simpleminded idiot," he uttered, his face contorted with his displeasure. "How could you be such a fool?"

Then Isobel knew what the lab technologist had not. This was what her dream had meant to convey, to liken the treachery of Angelo's own brother, his murderer and hers, to the perfidy of the Candless heirs, one of whom had betrayed the others. The only one who had nothing to lose by the addition of another heir. The one most horrified that Gina's murder had been arranged by one of them. The only one who could have paid fifty thousand dollars to buy a falsified paternity testing.

"Why, Bruce?" she asked softly. "Why did you do it?" But suddenly, she knew. Angelo tightened his fingers around hers. "Did you think that one final insult would finally convince your mother to leave him?"

"Dear God, no," Patrice moaned, looking at her eldest, at her pride and joy, the one with all the talent and wit and charisma. The only one who respected her. Her head shook. "No."

Candless turned on Isobel. "What the hell are you talking about?"

Angelo stepped forward, every cell of his being radiating danger in reprisal for the implied threat to

Isobel. "Maybe you'd like to rephrase, and address your question to your son."

Candless took an involuntary step backward, visibly gulping. He turned slowly, a quarter turn so that he could see his son. "What is she talking about, Bruce? What final insult?" His voice trembled with rage.

Bruce swore. "Kels is right, you know. You are a creep. You are a bully. You don't deserve to have a family." He turned to Patrice. "Mother—"

"No," she interrupted fiercely. "Don't say it. Don't you say it." She looked around at each of her children in turn, then demanded, "How could you do this? How could you? Conrad? Harry? Kelsey?"

Candless interrupted. "I'm talking to you now, Bruce."

"The question, Mother, is not how could they, but how could they not?" Bruce retorted, ignoring his father. "They're weaklings. They're fools. They are what he made them," Bruce shouted, pointing at his father. "Morally vacant! What kind of example did you set, staying with him? How many times did I beg you to leave him? Didn't I go out and earn my own fortune so you wouldn't have to stay? And here you sit, shaking like a damn leaf, still too afraid to be alone, to leave the man who destroyed us all, one after another."

Candless reared up and would have flown in his murderous rage at his son, but Angelo constrained him, forcing Candless back into his chair.

Patrice's head shook as if she were palsied, and a flat keening noise came from her throat. "Bruce, what have you done?"

"I set it up, Mother." He looked with loathing to

Isobel. "Gina was pregnant. She knew the father, but he had abandoned her. She needed help. I saw an opportunity to give you the excuse you needed to finally leave this bastard, and what does he do? He takes Gina's baby into the bosom of his family, and you just sit there doing your martyr act."

"How?" Candless asked dully. "How did you do it?"

"I bribed a lab tech, and she falsified the report. It was that simple. You see? Gina just wanted support for the baby, but she wouldn't have come to live here for any amount of money. What happened, Harry? How did you bait her into that death trap?"

"Oh, that was the real INS. Stand-up men, you know. They wanted a stoolie in Camp Candless. Conrad was in deep shit. I saw an opportunity, too, bro, to keep Connie and Sinjin out of trouble, and get rid of the old man's bastard brat all in one masterstroke."

Bruce stared at his brother in disgust. "How did you get her there?"

Harry laughed. "I couldn't have known Gina would have done anything not to come live among this happy little family, but it worked out quite well. She took the bait to that barrio death trap because she thought she could get what the INS wanted without having to live here, acting as their stoolie."

Bruce shook his head at Harry and the rest, his jaw cocked, his ire up. "Look at them, Mother. They would rather conspire to murder an innocent human being than to go out and take care of themselves."

Patrice broke. An unholy cry came out of her mouth. She stood, pulled her pearl-handled gun out from beneath her sweater, gripped it with both hands and pointed it at her husband of more than thirty years. "You!" she screeched. "You did this!"

She fired the gun, then fired again and again, wildly, all aimed at her husband. Isobel clutched the baby to her breast, turning toward Angelo, feeling the vibrations of the terrifying shots and Seth's screams to the center of her being.

Candless stood frozen behind his desk. In the first split second, Angelo deflected the trajectory of the bullet, then again and again, enraging Patrice who would fire until her husband lay dead.

And all that time, pain and grief and self-recrimination roaring in his head, those seconds stretched into an eternity, and Angelo saw how it was coming to pass that the fragmented images of Isobel's death were true.

The distraction, the desperation seized him, and when Patrice pulled the trigger one last time, he failed to deflect the bullet, which ricocheted off a brass sculpture on Ian Candless's desk, and headed straight for the head of Gina Sellers's baby.

Isobel saw the bullet coming at Seth, despite her protective posture. In her mind the fractured seconds passed as hours in which she knew that this was one bullet over which Angelo de Medici, Avenging Angel of the Lord, had no power whatsoever.

This was the moment of highest truth, the consequence of her choice to become human again to save the baby from his mother's fate.

This was the moment in which she was the most human, and the most terrified. She might choose, of her own free will, to turn and take the bullet herself to spare the baby for whom she had already given up everything else. She could choose between this life and any possibility of her union with Angelo, or she could choose her own death, because that was what it would take to protect Seth's life.

But there was only one choice, and they both knew it. As much as Angelo was an Avenging Angel in his soul, so was she a Guardian in hers. All the passion and commitment and love between them, centuries of it, were expressed in her cry to Angelo.

And then she turned and the bullet tore into her mortal body and entered her heart, and Isobel Avedon died.

Again.

THE INS AND HALF A DOZEN other city, state and federal agencies descended on the estate within a matter of an hour. Every member of the family was taken into custody for one crime or another. Conspiracy. Fraud. Bribery. Accessory. Murder, attempted and real.

Crippled in his grief and rage, Angelo cradled Seth to his shoulder with his right arm and Isobel's body in his left. None but one dared approach him in that eerie, silent aftermath, torn asunder only by Seth's heartrending cries. And that one was the Avenging Angel Pascal.

Unseen and unheard, he urged his dearest compatriot to let a woman from the Child Protective Services, brought in by helicopter, take charge of Seth.

Angelo's entire body shuddered. His human heart felt near to exploding. He had business to conduct, an appearance to make, reparations to demand in heaven, or he would never have let the baby go. But a bevy of guardians, Isobel's own kind, came to watch over the woman, and so Angelo surrendered the babe to her arms.

He lifted his beloved Isobel and carried her outside. The wind whipped high, the sea churned. His grief alone was cause enough to blacken the skies. His anger wrought fearsome bolts of lightning, but the only rain fell on the cheeks of Angelo de Medici.

He prepared himself to leave her lying in a protected cove on the beach. Her face was that of an angel, alabaster in death, more precious to him than the life of any other—now or ever. It was due to his ego, his unbending swaggering arrogant attitude, that Isobel lay dead again, and he could not tolerate the pain. He backed away from her body, leaving no prints in the wet sand, until the anguish forced him into his ethereal angelic form. He transcended the earth and soared to the heavens, his mighty wings spread hard and wide. And when he came before the heavenly council, he saw Pascal again, along with all the saints and martyrs, the powerful assembled to hear his demands.

He let them see him, in all his fierce glory—the Avenging Angel they knew so well—and then he collapsed his wings and stood before them with none of his power or radiant trappings. Instead, he demanded as a man that the life of Isobel Avedon be restored to her, along with the baby she had sacrificed herself to save.

"No one," he called out, "*no one* among us has answered a higher call than the Guardian Isobel Avedon. Haven't we stopped ages of tyranny? Haven't we defeated the forces of evil, time and again, throughout all the millennia? Will we not fight this battle as long as it takes? But, I say to you, the saving of one innocent life is as much as all of this. What is done to the least of God's children is done to the greatest. And this day, Isobel died to save the life of an innocent babe.''

He was reminded on high that these were Isobel's own consequences, the inevitable outcome of the free will she had chosen to exercise.

He argued on, creating a barrage of emotions, the equivalents of lumps in human throats and tears in human eyes, to every angel in the assembly. But, in the end, all his eloquence, his threat to resign the Avenging Angels, his defiance, his pleading, changed nothing.

He saw with terrible clarity the inevitability. He had promised her he would let nothing happen to Seth. He just hadn't known it would mean that she must die in the baby's stead.

He saw that it was true that there were none so tortured in heaven and earth as the Avenging Angels. Like him, in one degree or another, they had all suffered agonizing loss, and it was this that gave them their might and their mastery, their taste for reprisal. But for all his power to wreak the vengeance of the Lord, Angelo could not save Isobel's life.

What she had willingly sacrificed out of love, he could not take back in the name or interests of justice.

Pascal saw the knowledge sink like a knife into the heart of the Avenging Angel Angelo de Medici, and his own soul quaked with sorrow. ''Go back to her, *mon ami.* Go back to her now.'' And when he had gone, when he held Isobel's slight body on the beach in the gathering twilight of that fateful day, Pascal saw to it that the others understood this mighty transformation. Angelo had served mankind in all his fierce quest for justice for half a millennium, and yet when the time came, he gave up his pretensions and his attitudes and his arrogance, and he knew that it was love and not might that must—in the end—save the world.

Only, Pascal argued, there was nowhere in the annals of heaven or earth a love as powerful as Angelo's for his Isobel. He had learned the most important value of all, had he not?

As Pascal had suggested, Angelo returned to the beach where he had left Isobel's body.

His heart splintered as the last rays of sunlight appeared over the vast Pacific. He took Isobel's lifeless form into his aching, empty human arms and cradled her body to his own, and sank to his knees.

He learned that there were places in the human heart too deep, too impenetrable for tears to reach or heal, and so he had none. Simply a profound prayer that Isobel be spared this merciless death, which only his arrogant avenging attitude had made necessary at all, remained.

Seconds passed as hours, but it was not until Angelo conceded his powers, conceded his faults, conceded even Isobel's life, that her eyes fluttered open and her wound healed over as if no bullet had ever pierced her flesh and Isobel smiled for him, her lip caught between her teeth, her heart soaring with joy.

Isobel was alive again. Truly, mortally alive.

When his beautiful brown eyes filled with tears, she knew that he was truly, mortally alive as well, without his powers, and that he was hers for this lifetime. And that in the spectacular Vail valley of Colorado, they would raise Seth, and other babies as well, together.

HARLEQUIN®
INTRIGUE®

There's a small town in New Mexico where no one is who they seem to be...and everyone has a secret....

Welcome to...

FOUR WINDS

Join **Aimée Thurlo** as she takes you to a town of myth and mystery and introduces you to three men who make your pulse race....

Meet the Blackhorse brothers—
Gabriel, Joshua and Lucas—in

#427: HER DESTINY (JULY)
#441: HER HERO (NOVEMBER)
#458: HER SHADOW (MARCH 1998)

Come to Four Winds...the town where dreams come true.

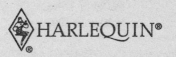

DELTA JUSTICE

A family dynasty of law and order
is shattered by a mysterious crime
of passion.

Don't miss the second Delta Justice book
as the mystery unfolds in:

Letters, Lies and Alibis
by Sandy Steen

Rancher Travis Hardin is determined to right a
sixty-year wrong and wreak vengeance on the Delacroix.
But he hadn't intended to fall in love doing it. Was his
desire for Shelby greater than his need to destroy her
family?

Lawyer Shelby Delacroix never does anything halfway.
She is passionate about life, her work...and Travis. Lost
in a romantic haze, Shelby encourages him to join her in
unearthing the Delacroix family secrets. Little does she
suspect that Travis is keeping a few secrets of his own....

Available in October
wherever Harlequin books are sold.

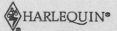

HARLEQUIN®

COMING NEXT MONTH

#441 HER HERO by Aimée Thurlo
Four Winds
Navajo healer Joshua Blackhorse was the one man who could help
Nydia Jim keep a promise to her son—and save a life. But when she
arrived in Four Winds she found Joshua accused of a terrible crime.

#442 HEART OF THE NIGHT by Gayle Wilson
Driven by a need she told herself was professional curiosity,
Kate August delved into the mystery of Thorne Barrington, the only
living victim of a serial bomber. But for what need did she follow him
into the darkness, determined to find the heart of the mystery…and
the man?

#443 A REAL ANGEL by Cassie Miles
Avenging Angels
It was Rafe Santini's job to stop an outbreak of a deadly virus.
Making love to his earthly assistant Jenna wasn't part of his duties. In
all his years as an Avenging Angel, Rafe had never been tempted by
the sins of the flesh. Why now, when so many lives were at stake?

#444 FAMILY TIES by Joanna Wayne
When Ashley's husband was nearly killed, she went into hiding,
taking with her the best part of Dillon Randolph—his baby. It took
three years for Dillon to find her and now he wanted her and his child
to come home to Texas. Surely now it'd be safe to be together
again…or was it?

AVAILABLE THIS MONTH:

#437 FATHER AND CHILD	**#439 BEFORE THE FALL**
Rebecca York	Patricia Rosemoor
#438 LITTLE GIRL LOST	**#440 ANGEL WITH AN ATTITUDE**
Adrianne Lee	Carly Bishop

Look us up on-line at: http://www.romance.net

Coming in August 1997!

THE BETTY NEELS
RUBY COLLECTION

August 1997—Stars Through the Mist
September 1997—The Doubtful Marriage
October 1997—The End of the Rainbow
November 1997—Three for a Wedding
December 1997—Roses for Christmas
January 1998—The Hasty Marriage

COLLECTOR'S EDITION

This August start assembling the
Betty Neels Ruby Collection. Six of the
most requested and best-loved titles have
been especially chosen for this collection.
From August 1997 until January 1998,
one title per month will be available to avid
fans. Spot the collection by the lush ruby red
cover with the gold Collector's Edition banner
and your favorite author's name—Betty Neels!

Available in August at your favorite retail outlet.

HARLEQUIN®